KILLED BY DEATH

13 Horror Stories by Matthew Weber

Content Warning

These are horror stories and are intended to horrify.

Contents

Prologue

Ever look back on your life and wonder, *What the heck was I thinking?* I experienced some of those moments while reviewing the tales for this collection. Some of these stories are a decade old, and each has previously appeared in an anthology or magazine, etc., as well as my now out-of-print collection *Seven Feet Under* (Sinister Grin Press, 2016). The only exception is a new tale titled *Silver Bullet Lies*, which I added for extra freshness.

Some of these stories are mean and nasty. I might have mellowed with age since I wrote them. Raising kids will do that to you. With that said, a good horror story should go for the throat, and the material you'll find in *Killed by Death* does not spare the blade. Judging from this collection, I must have been an angry young man.

These days, I'm a ray of sunshine.

-   M. Weber

Incident at the Buttered Biscuit

At the jingle of the diner's front door, Katy Clemmons popped out of the kitchen with notepad in hand. She plucked a pencil from behind her ear as a man in a dripping, black raincoat took a seat at the counter.

"Good afternoon," Katy greeted with a tip-friendly smile. Business was thin, and every little bit helped. "How are you, today?"

The man pulled back his hood. Dark circles cradled his eyes. He nodded with a grunt.

The Buttered Biscuit was a small, home-style diner that had a long countertop with a row of nine barstools. Four booths lined the glass front wall, each table covered with a red-and-white checkered cloth.

"I don't believe I've seen you in here before," Katy said.

He was the only customer. Beneath the coat he wore jeans and a gray, rain-speckled sweatshirt. Several days' worth of stubble peppered his face. Katy placed him in his mid to late twenties.

"It's been a while, I guess," he said in a hoarse voice.

"You live nearby?"

He wiped water from his brow. "Used to," he said.

"Used to? So you've moved away?"

He looked the place over. "Been gone for a while."

"For a while?" Katy said. "Does that mean you've moved back?"

After a moment he said, "Here for the time being. We'll see how it goes."

"I just moved here a month ago. Seems like a nice enough town. My mother inherited a house over on Haddon Road. You know where that is?"

"Yes. I do."

"Oh, good. Ours is the—" She stopped before describing her house's exact location to the stranger. Sometimes she talked too much when trying to be perky. "It was my grandfather's place. My mom's dad. He died of a heart attack."

The man lifted a book of matches from an ashtray on the counter. He flipped it over, studied the diner's logo on the back then tucked it into his coat pocket.

"Anyway, the house beats the heck out of our old apartment," Katy said. "That place was like living in a shoebox. Here's the menu. What can I get you to drink?"

"Coffee, please."

"Sure thing. Cream or sugar?"

"No, thanks."

"One black coffee coming right up."

The man's sunken eyes and sullen demeanor reminded Katy of her father, a manic depressive with a drinking problem. A fireman by trade, Jeffrey Clemmons had a good heart but a heavy head. She'd found him dead one afternoon upon returning home from high school in the spring of her junior year. Sprawled across his recliner, his face a cold blue, he'd overdosed on a cocktail of Jack Daniels and painkillers. No more bear hugs from Daddy. Say goodbye to the father-daughter dance at your wedding.

The man yawned, and Katy lifted the carafe. "Long night?" she asked.

"You could say that."

She shook her head. "I know how that goes. Like my mom always says, you can't overstate the importance of a good night's rest."

He raised his head from his hands. "That's what I hear."

Katy filled the cup and placed it on a saucer in front of him.

"I'd love a good night's rest," he said.

"What's the problem? Trouble sleeping?"

The man slowly sipped the coffee. His long face looked weary and wounded, almost haunted. "Only when I close my eyes," he said with a weak smile that didn't quite materialize.

Katy nodded. "My dad suffered from insomnia." She thought for a moment then extended him a hand. "I'm Katy. Katy Clemmons."

He hesitated, then folded his fingers around hers and squeezed gently. "My name is Ronald."

She gave another cheerful smile. "Ronald McDonald?" she asked in hope of lightening his mood.

"Ronald Burch."

Katy let go of his hand. She'd moved to Shady Brake from two towns away, but everyone in the whole county knew that name, and the nasty little rhyme it had inspired.

Ronald Burch burnt down a church while everyone was in it. In a battle of evil with the devil himself, Ronald Burch would win it.

"You've heard of me?"

Katy opened her mouth but didn't know what to say. She pinched her lips between her teeth.

"Yeah," he said. "You've heard of me."

She remembered Alton in the back, rolling out dough for pies, and thanked heaven she wasn't stuck here alone with Ronald Burch.

"I'm not a monster," he said. "I know that's what you're thinking. You and everybody else."

Katy forced herself to stop staring at the customer, turned on her heels and went to the kitchen to collect her thoughts.

Alton was pressing a sheet of dough into a pan. A heavy balding man in an apron and a hair net, he pinched the edges of the pie crust into a lacey frill. "Everything okay up front?" he asked.

Calm down, she thought. *Ronald Burch has done absolutely nothing to you.* "Yes, everything's fine."

His order! Katy slapped her forehead. She stepped back into the lobby and asked, "Can I get you anything to eat?"

The diner's radio always played the oldies station. T-Bone Walker's "They Call it Stormy Monday" hummed softly from the speakers.

Ronald Burch took a long sip of coffee and met her eyes. "I'm not sick anymore," he said. "I came back home to start over, if people will forgive me."

Momentarily frozen, she eventually said, "The patty melt is delicious."

His gaze fell away, releasing her from its grip. "I'll take the patty melt."

"Fries with that?" she asked with a mouth full of cotton.

"Sure."

The bright lights and familiar smells of the kitchen eased her nerves.

"One patty melt," she told Alton.

"Whaddya know," he said. "Sounds like we have a customer."

Katy gave a low whistle. "And one heck of a customer." She told him the name. Alton stopped prepping the food. A grave expression passed over him like a shadow.

"Here at the Biscuit?"

She flipped up her palms. "All I know is that he's sitting at the counter, drinking our coffee."

Alton walked to the service window and peeked into the lobby. He mouthed the words *holy shit*.

Ten years ago, the story plastered the headlines. According to reports, the Burch family had attended Shady Brake Evangelical Church. Martin and Eleanor Burch were strict puritanical parents who'd been experiencing severe behavioral problems with their son. It came to a head during one Sunday morning sermon, in which Ronald, having excused himself for the restroom, soaked every exit with a can of kerosene, trickling a stream outside like a fuse. He bound the door handles with chains from the church's swing set, and lit the whole place up. The congregation panicked, trampling each other in the melee. A small sanctuary, the building quickly filled with smoke and fire. The people inside pounded the doors, screaming and asphyxiating, begging for God's mercy.

Katy's dad was one of the first firemen to the scene. As his engine pulled up, someone in the church smashed a stained-glass window, trying to escape. He'd told how the blood-curdling screams that escaped the inferno had haunted him from that day forward. Sixty-two people died. Sixty-two men, women and children were viciously murdered.

The police had found Ronald Burch watching the whole ghastly ordeal from a nearby tree. He was perched on a branch, snacking on unleavened bread and communion wine.

"It's really him, isn't it?" Katy asked Alton. "I thought they'd locked him in an institution."

Alton pulled away from the window and folded his hands together. Katy had never seen him so grim and brooding, eyes smoldering beneath his brow.

"I heard they'd released him," he said in a hushed voice. "But we didn't think he'd ever show his face around here again."

Katy realized that Alton, born and raised in Shady Brake, had likely been acquainted with the victims. Maybe even related.

"I'll whip up the sandwich," he said. "You keep him here." He walked to the telephone.

Katy stepped back into the lobby. The steep angle with which Ronald Burch tilted back his cup told Katy it was empty.

"Refill?"

"Please," he said.

She poured the coffee, watching the steam snake up from the mug.

"I got back home two nights ago," he said. "My grandmother took me in. Didn't have anywhere else to go. Been keeping my head down, since I'm not very popular around here."

Katy conjured an image of Burch standing outside the diner, splashing the plate-glass with a kerosene can, the fuel streaming down and shimmering. Trapped inside, she begged for her life as he laughed and flicked a lit match, igniting the building into a cage of flame.

"I probably wouldn't really know," she stammered. "Like I said, I'm new here."

"But you know the story."

"Everybody knows that story."

"Do you believe in mental illness?"

Katy's head began to hurt. "Of course I do."

"Do you believe people who've suffered from mental illness can be cured? Be rehabilitated?"

She thought of her father and how she had been so furious that he'd given up hope. He had succumbed to his demons even though Katy knew deep down that he could have overcome them if only he had put forth the necessary effort. If he had only tried harder... She looked at Burch. "Yes."

The muscles in his face relaxed, as if a noose around his neck had loosened a notch. "Thank you for saying that."

"Do you regret what you did?"

For a long moment he stared out the window, into the overcast sky and the haze of a steady drizzle. "Every waking second," he said. "And I never really sleep."

A searing pain bit her hand. The coffee pot she held had tilted and spilled on her. "Dammit!" She set it aside and grabbed a handful of napkins to clean the mess from the floor.

"What do you mean, you never sleep?" Katy knelt down and wiped the tile. She tossed the dirty towels into the trash can.

"All I hear is screaming." His voice broke up. "Those poor people in the church. Screaming for help. Dying from my hand. Burning alive. That's all I hear when I close my eyes." The gleam of his tears caught the light.

The massacre played out in Katy's mind like the trailer of some sick midnight movie. The bound doors of the church buckled with the blows of panicked parishioners. Smoke billowed from broken windows as charred limbs smashed the colored glass to flee the raging blaze.

She released a deep breath that she hadn't realized she'd been holding. "I'm sorry to hear that."

"No, I'm sorry." Burch blotted his face with his sleeve. "I shouldn't unload on you like that. It's just that you didn't seem to immediately hate me."

Katy looked at the floor. "I've seen mental illness up close. Sometimes people need help, or they do terrible things."

"*Patty melt!*" Alton shouted from the back.

"Your food's ready. I'll be back in a minute." She pushed through the double doors of the kitchen.

The greasy burger and melted cheese were sliding off the rye bread. Alton dumped a pile of crinkle-cut fries onto the plate and shoved it across the table to Katy.

"It's full of rat poison," he said without a trace of humor.

"It is not."

"It oughtta be. You're not getting chummy with him, are you? He's the most hated man in this entire town. He is pure evil. You better keep your distance."

Katy raised an eyebrow. "Um, *duh*. He's a mass murderer. We're not bosom buddies. But I'm his waitress. What am I supposed to do? Communicate psychically?"

"Well, there's the asshole's sandwich. I hope he chokes on it."

The little bell above the diner door chimed from the lobby. As Katy gathered Ronald Burch's napkins and silverware, she heard it jingle again.

She walked out of the kitchen with his food. The Platters were crooning "Smoke Gets in Your Eyes" from the radio.

Ronald Burch was no longer alone.

Four tall men hovered near a booth to his left, each wearing woven ski masks. Two leaned against the counter, the others stood with their arms crossed. Dressed in denim and flannel, they had thick limbs and wore heavy work boots.

The door opened, and two more men entered with their faces concealed. The shining headlights of a pickup cut through the gloom outside. The truck pulled into the parking lot on the other side of the glass. Both occupants pulled ski masks over their heads as they stepped out of the truck into the rain. The door jingled again.

Not a word was spoken.

Hands trembling, Katy quietly placed the food on the counter in front of Burch as if nothing were out of the ordinary. "One patty melt and fries," she whispered.

His unshaven face was bloodless, whiskers dark against the pale skin. The bags beneath his eyes seemed to cave into his hollow cheeks. "What'd you do?" he asked Katy.

"Nothing," she said, stunned at the suggestion.

"Did you call some sort of mob?" he said with a tremor in his voice, glancing over his shoulder. "Is that what this is?"

"I swear I didn't."

The group of four murmured amongst themselves and motioned to the men by the door.

A spot of color in the gray outdoors caught Katy's attention. In a puddle on the asphalt, just outside the diner, was a large, bright red jug.

"So you're just like everyone else," Burch said to Katy.

"No." She put a hand to her cheek. "I'm not."

Like a pack of wolves, the men grabbed him and wrenched him from his seat. He smacked to the floor with a yelp. They were all over him.

"Leave him alone!" Katy shouted.

Two men pinned him down while the others punched and stomped. The fists drew up and shot back down.

"Get off me!" Burch cried in a strangled voice. *"Get the hell off!"*

Katy lost sight of him in a maelstrom of elbows and boot heels.

"Quit hurting him!" She lunged over the counter and slapped at the men's backs. The patty melt plate shattered on the tile. *"Stop it!"*

They ignored her and dragged him to the door.

"I'm sorry!" pleaded Burch as he slid kicking and flailing across the floor. "I'm better now! *I'm rehabilitated!"*

With a jingle, they pushed through the door and pulled him into the parking lot. Katy dashed outside, slapping and cursing the men. She clawed the back of the closest one, but two meaty arms wrapped around her.

"Stay out of it!" Alton said in her ear. "Don't get involved!"

"They can't do this!" Katy twisted and kicked, the rain in her eyes clouding her sight.

"He's a monster," Alton said. "He owes a heavy price to a lot of people."

Burch curled into a ball as the masked men circled around, crushing his body with their heavy boots. They ripped off his raincoat, and two smashed him with aluminum bats.

One of them grabbed the gas can and twisted off the lid.

"This is *insane!*" Katy howled as the man doused the fuel onto Burch, who shuddered on the ground and begged for mercy.

A Zippo flipped open, then a spark.

With a *whoosh*, Ronald Burch burst into flames. His piercing scream shook Katy to the bowels. Like a knife to the ear, his death-throe shrieking snuffed out all other sound and rattled her brain, quaking inside her with punishing force.

"*Noooooo,*" she gasped, tears streaming.

Burch writhed in a blanket of flickering fire, rolling around, batting uselessly at his melting flesh as his shrill, shattering pitch fell to a harsh, dry croak. Finally, his body went still, hissing and popping like bacon in a skillet. The sight of it seared into Katy's mind like a branding iron.

She slid down, and Alton released her. She fell to her knees and bent over, sobbing as the blackened corpse steamed in the light rain.

When the smell hit her, she fainted.

***

"Looks like they're hiring over at the Huddle House," Katy's mother said three weeks later, as they pored over the newspaper classifieds. "Oh, wait. Night shift only. You don't want that."

"I'll take night shift," Katy said, resting her head in her hands. They both sat at the kitchen table.

"Honey, you need to get some rest before you pick up any night work. You look so peaked."

Katy glanced at her reflection in a chrome toaster on the countertop, at her eyes recessed into dark hollows. She looked like she'd aged five years since the incident at the Buttered Biscuit. "I'll be okay," she said with a sigh. "Sleep doesn't seem to be in the cards these days."

"You have to sleep, dear. You can't overstate the importance of a good night's rest. I know you've been through a lot, but I really wish you could put that awful mess behind you. Still having nightmares about the diner?"

Katy looked outside the kitchen window. Rain was falling again, and the sickening pitch of Ronald Burch's tortured wails echoed somewhere deep within her.

"Only when I close my eyes."

The End

Dammit, Mavis

Earl Ketchum sat in a rocking chair on his front porch. He sipped iced tea, breathed the fresh Alabama air, and watched the lightning bugs flicker as he plotted to kill his brother-in-law.

Earl's sister Mavis had always been homely and slow-witted. She would swoon at the very thought of someone, anyone, asking for her hand in matrimony. Franky Gubler seized the opportunity, marrying her as soon as she'd squeaked through high-school. Earl didn't see the appeal, but Franky was nearly brain-dead himself. At twenty-six years old, the guy had been divorced twice and spawned three kids he neglected. But Mavis, bless her heart, swore that their holy union would be the exception that turned Franky around.

"I love him, Earl, and love is all that matters," she'd told her brother when he'd pointed out Franky's long list of shortcomings. Earl had breached the conversation after stewing over the news of Franky's proposal.

"You'll have a stupid last name," Earl said. "*Gubler*."

"I don't mind."

"Did he give you a ring?" They'd been sitting on the couch in her trailer, him smoking a Doral as she folded a stack of Franky's ratty briefs. There was no jewelry on her hand.

"No, but he gave me his word."

"His word?"

"Yes, that his love would be eternal."

Where she had seen hope, Earl saw Franky's empty promises. And then the lousy son-of-a-bitch had gone and beaten her up. Currently out on another bender, Prince

Charming had left his new bride at home with two fresh black eyes. Mavis had phoned Earl and told him the story, and he'd dashed over to help. The sight of his sister swollen and crying had sealed Franky Gubler's fate. Earl wasn't going to stand idly by while someone beat on a Ketchum—thick-headed or not. Mavis was kin, and that's all that mattered.

Earl finished his tea. He decided that Franky Gubler was a piece of crap and deserved to be treated as such, so he stepped into the house to fetch his truck keys.

As he pulled into the lot of the Rusty Hinge, Earl saw the dilapidated Camaro parked outside the bar. Franky was inside, getting sloshed as usual. Booze: His true eternal love. Earl knew things would get rowdy if he confronted him inside, and that the bartender would probably call the law. It'd be better to bide his time, so he sat in his truck in a dimly lit corner of the lot, smoking cigarettes and watching the entrance for the moment Franky walked out with a gut full of suds.

***

"What the hell is that?" Earl had asked that question a month ago.

"Ain't she a beaut?" Mavis bent over the massive catfish as she slit open its belly with a tarnished filet knife. Its glistening body nearly covered the entire top of the picnic table. "Not even close to the biggest one out there, either. At least, that's what Franky says." A yellow egg-sack squirted out of the open gash into the pool of blood that dripped through the gaps in the boards.

It had been the evening of their engagement party. Franky and his drunken friends were yukking it up around the keg, while Mavis tended to the cooking detail.

"That is far and away the biggest freshwater fish I've ever seen," Earl said.

"Franky said he and Bubba Taylor found it nesting in the shallows, but they were too scared to noodle for it. They both had to gaff it to drag it on the bank. Then shot it with a pistol." Mavis stretched a flap of rubbery gray skin with a pair of pliers as she worked the underside with the tip of her blade, cutting the membrane to separate the white meat. "Not too sure how fresh the water is, though…" she said with a grin.

Earl gave her a prying look. "What do you mean?"

"Franky says the cats got real big like this because he's giving them super-food."

"What super-food? Where'd he catch this thing?" On further inspection, Earl saw that this was no ordinary catfish. It had four eyes—a pair on each side—and rather than thin, black whiskers, it had six thick tentacle-like appendages that flanked its maw. He leaned closer and saw tiny suction cups on the underside of each one. The creature's jaws were lined with inch-long teeth, the size and span of a bear-trap.

"Remember the Green Hole, down at the end of Shady Brake Road? Where we used to fish as kids?"

Earl remembered it well. A quiet and secluded trail through the woods led to a pond-size swell in Limestone Creek. The deep and green water, the peaceful seclusion, that scenic retreat had been one of his favorite spots when growing up. But there was a good reason he didn't fish there anymore, and Franky Gubler was the guilty party.

"This ain't a normal fish, Mavis."

"Well, I know that, silly. It's a dadgum blue-ribbon prize winner, is what it is."

"It's some kind of mutant. I ain't eating that. You shouldn't either."

"Oh, Earl. Don't be such a worry-wart."

On the days when he showed up for work, Franky made his meager living driving a pump truck for a septic-tank cleaning service. Earl had hiked to the Green Hole a couple years ago and discovered the pump truck backed up to the water. Franky was emptying the vile contents of the tank right into the pond, polluting all the life and wonders of nature. He'd been known to take jobs "off the books" like cleaning up chemical contamination from a holding pond at the paper plant, or sucking up spilled fertilizer from an overturned truck on Bill Watson's farm. No doubt he'd been dumping all that junk into Earl's favorite fishing spot, rendering it unusable. Earl had hated Franky from that day forward, and that was long before the guy had ever laid a hand on his sister.

"That stupid asshole is still dumping his shit in the creek?!" he said to his sister.

She shrugged. "It saves us a lot of gas and driving time, since he ain't gotta make the trip across town to the sanitation depot. And I don't see what it hurts."

"What it hurts? Dammit, Mavis, that water eventually makes it into the drinking supply. And he's dumping God-knows-what kind of filth into it."

"The city cleans the water, Earl."

"Yeah, well, that water's got a long ways to go before it gets to the treatment plant. I mean, for cryin' out loud, just look what happened to that fish!"

Mavis glanced at the mangled carcass and then looked at him cockeyed. "That's a whole lot of meat, big brother. I don't see what the problem is. We all get to eat for free!" She gave him a smile as she cut the flesh into strips to be battered.

Earl shook his head. "Count me out. I'll swing by the Burger Hut on the way home."

***

The double doors of the Rusty Hinge slung open and two women walked outside, chuckling over their shoulders at Franky who staggered behind them, cat-calling and whistling. They hurried away from him, got in their car and locked the doors. He stood outside their vehicle for a moment, teetered back and forth, then gave up and headed for his Camaro.

As the ladies drove out of the parking lot, Earl crept out of his pickup with a hickory baseball bat tight in his grip.

"Hey, buddy, got a light?"

When Franky turned to see who'd spoken, the bat smacked his head with full driving force. He spun around and went down like a felled tree.

The impact had enough power to vibrate through the wood and sting Earl's palms. He poked his brother-in-law in the back with the Louisville Slugger. The body didn't stir. With the parking lot clear, Earl ditched the bat, grabbed Franky beneath the shoulders and hauled him into the truck bed. He slammed the tailgate and climbed into the cab. With a squeal of the tires, Earl peeled away from the Rusty Hinge.

***

Earl watched Franky stir to life, grumbling and moaning, wrists tied behind his back, his legs bound at the ankles with sturdy rope. The night simmered with the sound of croaking toads and chirping crickets.

"My head ... God, it hurts."

Leaning against a tree, Earl remained silent as Franky squirmed in the bed of the truck, trying to gauge his whereabouts. Then Earl lit a cigarette.

"Who's there? Why am I tied up?" Franky, on the verge of sobbing, went still and held his breath.

Earl figured the implications of his brother-in-law's current predicament must be dawning on him.

"What do you want?" Franky said in a shaky voice. "You want money? I can pay you. I can get money, I swear."

The lie amused Earl.

"Who are you? Why are you doing this?" Franky said. "Where'd you bring me?"

"You can't tell by the smell?"

"Who's that? *Earl?* Earl, is that you?"

Earl gave a dry laugh and shook his head. "You were always half retarded. But beating up Mavis ... I guess that was the dumbest thing you've ever done. 'Cause just look at the pickle you're in now."

"Mavis? Look, Earl, I can explain..."

Earl stepped out of the shadows. With the cig in his teeth, he reached over the sidewall and gripped Franky by the belt and shirt collar. He slid his body off the tailgate, and Franky thumped to the muddy ground with a sharp cry.

"Dammit, Earl! Listen! It ain't what you think!"

"The Ketchums don't take kindly to someone knocking around our females." Earl booted Franky in the side, rolling him over to the creek bank.

"I lost my temper, Earl! You would have, too!"

"So, I'm gonna sink you right down into this big toilet you created, just like another turd from your septic truck."

"*No!* Stop it! I've got to tell you some—"

Another kick to the ribs cut him off. Franky rolled to the edge of the water.

"Don't do this, Earl!"

Earl bent down, scooped him up and heaved Franky into the Green Hole with a splash. The water churned throughout the pond, signaling that whatever lay beneath had been disturbed. Struggling to stand upright and keep his head above water, Franky stirred the water to a froth.

"She was cheating on me!" He gagged on the filthy liquid. "With that asshole Bubba Taylor!"

Earl puffed out a cloud of smoke. "What'd you say?"

"I caught 'em in the act, Earl! Bubba had her buck-naked on the couch, humpin' away right in our own home!"

Earl squinted his eyes and thought hard about what he'd just heard. *Was Franky lying?* The Ketchums looked down on infidelity, and if what he said was true, it certainly shuffled the deck.

"That's why I hit her!" he said. "Bubba got a black eye, too! I lost my temper! What would you've done?" He coughed and slipped below the surface, only to bob back up and beg.

Mavis hadn't mentioned her cheating, and Earl didn't like being manipulated.

He retrieved a rope from the truck. Gripping one end tightly, he tossed a loop into the water, where it floated in front of Franky. Earl shined a flashlight on it and said, "I ain't getting in that water. Bite onto the rope, and I'll pull you to shore."

Franky stopped thrashing. "I just felt something move in here." His expression went blank. His pallor went white. "Against my leg. Something big."

"Then you'd better bite the rope."

The pond all around him began to swirl and bubble.

Franky looked at Earl. "Something's in the water!" he gasped. "Oh *shit!* Something's in here with me!"

"Probably a really huge fish."

"Ow… *Ow,* dammit! My leg!" His thrashing returned with a vengeance.

"The rope," Earl said. "You might oughtta hurry."

"I feel 'em. There's more than one," he whimpered. "They're all around me ... *Help me, Earl!*"

The surface exploded with a shower, and three mammoth creatures arose with a hungry hiss. Franky's face shriveled with terror. Slick with slime, they lunged onto him from all sides. Writhing tentacles wrapped his neck and head. He shrieked as they sunk their needle teeth into his flesh.

Earl staggered backward, in awe of the beasts in the beam of his light. Hideous monsters, the size of cattle, they had clusters of inky eyes and suckered tendrils that grappled their prey. Spiny dagger-like barbels armed the corners of their jaws. They ate Franky alive as they pulled him down, blood blooming in the water. His screams gurgled up from the murky creek.

And then there was calm. The water rippled quietly. An owl hooted in the distance. And the crickets and toads gradually resumed their singing.

"Dang," said Earl.

***

The next day, Mavis was hanging her laundry on the clothesline when Earl pulled up in his truck.

He stalked up to her, felt like yelling, but said nothing. He pulled out a box of Dorals and tapped them against his palm, packing the tobacco. He lit up the cigarette and let it dangle from his lip as he stood watching her.

She ignored him for a while but eventually said, "What is it, Earl? It ain't polite to stare."

He flicked the butt to the ground. "I don't appreciate being lied to, Mavis."

Mavis pinned a sheet to the line and flashed him her puppy-dog expression, the contrite look she'd used as a kid when Earl would catch her stealing his Moon Pies. "I didn't really *lie*, Earl. I just didn't tell you everything."

"Like how you was cheating on your husband?"

"That didn't give Franky the right to hit me!"

"That may be true, but you didn't have the right to *cheat*, either! That ain't how Ketchums behave!" Earl kicked at the dirt and lowered his voice. "You used me."

"I'm in love with Bubba," said Mavis, "and love is all that matters."

Earl rubbed his forehead, which was beginning to ache. Bubba Taylor: a lazy jackass who barely knew his ABCs.

"It's all because of you that I killed an innocent man."

"Innocent?" Mavis said. "Wasn't nothing innocent about Franky Gubler. You did right, Earl. I knew you would. He got what he had coming."

Back home on his porch, relaxing in his rocking chair, Earl thought about what Mavis had told him. Maybe she wasn't quite as dim as he'd figured.

He remembered how, as a kid, he'd spent many long hours sitting on the bank of the Green Hole with a bob on his line, hoping for the tug of a crappie or bass. Maybe he'd even land a "monster" catfish.

Those days were long gone, now, because of what Franky had done to the water ... and because of what now lived *in* the water. Earl knew the Green Hole streamed right back into Limestone Creek, which snaked another mile or two before emptying into Lake Matheson. With summer right around the corner, countless families would be swimming and boating in that lake every sunny weekend.

As the first lightning bug of the evening sparkled in the distance, Earl sipped his iced tea and decided that Mavis was right about one thing. Franky Gubler had been no innocent man.

The End

Code Black

We'd had problems with the Carrington family in the past, but nothing like this.

Officer Garcia and I stood alongside the principal of Trapper Valley High, as we all studied the large circle of blood painted on the floor of the gymnasium.

"Creepy as hell," said Garcia. New to the force, he'd only dealt with shoplifters and drunk drivers. He'd been told the stories of this town, but some things a man had to see for himself. "I ain't ever seen anything like this before."

The blood formed a ring in the middle of the basketball court, and in its center lay the severed head of a deer. A nine-point buck. Scrawled along the inner edge of the circle were strange black markings and symbols I didn't recognize.

This was the school my daughter Anna attended.

"The Carrington boy did this?" I asked.

Principal Phillips pursed her lips and nodded.

"Call Klein," I told Garcia. "Tell him it's a Code Blue." That was our signal for a weird situation.

Garcia rubbed his goatee and muttered something in Spanish, then stepped away and dialed the chief.

I felt Principal Phillips' stare linger on me with a dozen unspoken questions. A stern black woman who ran the school at the point of a ruler, she expected a lot from her students as well as from everyone else. But I didn't know what these markings meant.

"Well?" she prodded.

"Looks strange," I said.

"No kidding. What's it supposed to mean? It's a threat, isn't it? It's like he marked the school, right? He's targeting us for something."

"It doesn't appear to be friendly, I'll give you that." I knelt closer to the circle and tried to make out anything legible in the markings. No such luck. Although, I did find a charred slip of paper. On it: a photo of a shoulder and a shirt collar. The face had been burned away. Judging from its size, shape and the black-and-white photography, I guessed it to be a yearbook photo snipped out of a page. "What's the kid's name again? Luke?"

"Duke. He wasn't very sly about hiding whatever he was doing. Some of the other students caught sight of him in here during first period when there's no PE class."

"Duke Carrington…" I said. "Sounds like a cowboy's name. Or a singer's."

"Doesn't look like a cowboy to me," Phillips said, extending her smartphone to me. "Here's a video."

Of course, there's a video. Kids today…

I watched it. The shaky picture was shot with the screen held vertically, which didn't afford a very clear view, but apparently a crowd of students confronted the guy as he etched the writings with what looked like a charred tree branch. The other teens were pointing and laughing at him, calling him every name in the book.

"What are you doing, freak? You fuckin' weirdo! … Dookie, you done gone looney like the rest of your family? … Take a picture! Take a picture! … Puke Carrington! Holy shit you're getting kicked out of school for this!"

As they approached him, the lanky, curly-haired boy in the circle hardly reacted, remaining crouched over the floor, feverishly scribing out the symbols using black ashes from a small, smoldering pile. The camera drew closer, and he finally peered up into the lens with cold hatred in his eyes—eyes encircled with the wet, red blood of the deer.

"Holy shit, motherfucker's gone crazy!" howled one of the kids, then the screen went dead.

Phillips slid the phone into her coat pocket. "One of the kids put it on Youtube."

"Wonderful…" This means the phone at the station will be ringing off the hook. "What happened when the video cut off? Any physical confrontation?"

"No. The other students said that's when he stood up and pulled the deer head out of a plastic bag. That's when they got scared. And they're not usually scared of him. See, the kid is from over in Shady Brake, and his family– well, they struggle financially – so some of the other students tend to give him a hard time. They're used to him shying away from *them*, not the other way around."

I'd once arrested Duke's father for public intox and on another occasion for beating his wife. Duke's mother was no prize herself, a total pill-zombie. But nobody deserves to be abused, and when Mr. Carrington wasn't at home to knock her around, Duke's older brother would step in on his behalf. Just a month ago, Garcia had booked 18-year-old Vince Carrington for beating up his own mom—like father, like son, I guess.

It must be hell growing up in a place like that.

"So, he was bullied," I told her, "for being poor."

Phillips sighed and looked down.

I was from Shady Brake, too, and remembered exactly what it felt like to be ridiculed for what you didn't have … and how angry it could make you. "But there was no fight this morning?"

She shook her head. "According to the students, he just raised the deer, stared up at the ceiling, and recited some words in another language. Then, he walked out of the circle and right out of the gym without another word. No one has seen him since. We assume he left campus."

"Chief Klein's on the way," Garcia said, returning to the circle.

"Take some photos of the scene," I told him. "Get samples of the blood. Hell, I'm not sure how we're going to write this up. Vandalism? Hunting out of season? I assume the school wants to press charges?"

Phillips batted her eyelids, nervous. I could tell she didn't want to pile onto the kid's problems. Teenagers were a volatile bunch. I lived with one of my own. You didn't want to add to their angst, but you couldn't let them run wild, either. And some of them could be dangerous.

"I feel like we have to," she answered. "I mean, his actions show signs of a troubled mind. The boy needs help. And there's no other way to see this than as a threat to the other students. The safest move is to turn the matter over to the authorities. I don't want the boy back here until he's had counseling."

I thought of Anna sitting at a desk in some other room of this very campus, wearing her bookish glasses and a neat, straight ponytail. I pictured her writing in her journal, a reporter-to-be honing her craft for a bright future. Behind her, I saw a lanky kid emerge in the doorway and cast a shadow over her. He had curly hair, red eyes and carried a deer head, blood dripping from the stump of its neck. He stalked up to my daughter, and she never saw him coming.

I let out a deep breath and said, "I don't want him back here, either."

***

Again, I tapped on the window. Parked in the driveway of the Carringtons' trailer, Duke's mother, Mercy

Carrington, sat in the front passenger seat of a Bondo-covered Ford Taurus with her head against the glass. She appeared to be asleep. I knocked a third time, when her son Vince stepped outside the trailer door with two stuffed duffle bags hanging from his arms.

"Going on a trip?" I asked him.

"Can I help you?" he answered.

"Maybe. I'm looking for your brother."

He had a low-brow scowl and muscular arms that looked like they could do real damage when throwing a punch into his mother's ribs.

"He ain't here." He stepped off the stoop toward the car then hoisted the bags onto the trunk, staring at me in wait of the next question.

"Know where he's at?"

"He took off," Vince said.

"Where to?"

"Don't know."

"Why'd he run off?"

"I don't know." Vince looked down the road. "But I reckon *you* do..."

"You don't know *anything*?"

He threw me that scowl again. "I know things. But I don't know nothing that's gonna help *you*."

"Maybe you'd be helping your brother."

"Maybe I don't give a damn about my brother, or about helping the goddamn Trapper Valley P.D., either." He gave me a big grin like he had shit between his teeth and wanted to show it off.

"I'm sorry he did what he did," spoke a frail voice from the car. Mercy Carrington cranked down the window in front of me. "I'm sorry, officer. I told him not to mess with that stuff. Told him it was dangerous. Nobody 'round here listens to me."

Around forty-five years old, Mercy looked closer to sixty. She had stringy hair and pale, waxy skin, a hangdog face and drug-hazed eyes which always squinted, like direct sunlight might blind her. She spoke as though it took great physical effort, straining out the words with long sighs.

"What *stuff* are you talking about?" I asked her. "Your son got himself into some real trouble at school, ma'am. And we've got some questions for him down at the station. Can you tell me where he's at?"

She shook her head in a visible daze.

"He was caught vandalizing the gym," I said, as Vince slid a key into the Taurus' trunk and popped the hatch. "The principal believes he was leaving a message—some kind of threat to the school. She's worried he means to harm the other students."

"She's worried?" Mercy said with a lilt in her voice. "Well, don't that just beat all? She's worried he's gonna hurt those other sons-of-bitches who make the poor boy's life a living hell… Bless her heart. Tell me, Mr. Officer. Where have you been every time he's gotten his ass kicked by the bastards in his gym class? Seems like you had plenty of opportunity since it happens every fuckin' day!"

Mercy was showing the most spunk I'd ever seen from her tired junkie ass.

"But nooooo," she said. "The only time we see your face is when one of you motherfuckers show up to throw somebody from our family in jail."

"Tell him, Mama," Vince cheered. He slammed the trunk closed, having loaded the bags.

"To answer your question, *no*," she said, "I *don't* know where he is, and if I did, I wouldn't tell you. For a minute there, I was feeling sorry for what y'all had coming to you, but I wasn't thinking straight. Y'all don't care about nobody but yourselves, and you damn sure don't care about us."

Vince opened the door and slid into the driver's seat.

"The way you're talking," I said, "it sounds like what your son wrote on that gym floor *was* a threat. What is he threatening to do?"

"No, see, you got it all wrong, Mr. Policeman." She gave me a drowsy smile. "He didn't leave a threat for you people. He left a doorway. And not a door for you … a door for something else."

"For what?"

Vince started the car, and Mercy cranked up the window. "Devil only knows," she said. "Devil only knows … that's why we're leavin' town for a few days. Leave the mess to y'all."

As the car pulled out of the gravel driveway, a crackle came from the radio in my cruiser. I walked over and reached through the window for the speaker.

"Daniels here," I said.

"Ritch, it's Klein. I'm at the high school. I need you back this way. Situation has escalated. We've got a Code Red. I repeat, we've got a Code Red."

I thought of Anna, and my mouth went dry as hay. I hit the siren and blazed a trail back toward TVHS.

Code Red meant things had gotten dangerous.

***

Halfway there, my mobile buzzed with a text message from Anna.

What's happening on campus? Saw the Carrington video. School on lockdown now. Nobody knows why. Not even teachers. What's the SCOOP???

I weaved the cruiser through traffic and blasted past three red lights. A school on lockdown … my mind raced with horrific national headlines, and I saw two stark words like blood on cotton—*Active Shooter*. The damned, dreaded phrase that all too often accompanied news of a lockdown. Sandy Hook, Uvalde, and now Trapper Valley, too … All human tragedies put into motion because some asshole kids thought it'd be fun to antagonize their awkward peers—a teenage tradition as American as apple pie. Visions of assault rifles and high-capacity magazines flashed through my head.

Please God, let it be something else.

I'd endured my own schoolyard bullies years ago, and remembered how I dreaded crossing paths with one particular shithead named Clay Quimby. That prick took great joy in my humiliation. He'd nicknamed me "trailer trash," and once even dumped a garbage can full of urine on me while I was occupying a bathroom stall. For that, I'd hated his ever-loving guts. But enough to kill him? … Maybe.

Klein's Bronco was parked in front of the gymnasium along with every other vehicle on the force. Two officers flanked the building's door, and others stood guard at each corner of the campus, securing the perimeter.

I screeched to a stop and ran over to Klein. "Fill me in."

I recognized his expression—those narrowed eyes and two pondering thought lines halving his brow beneath the brim of his hat. He saw scattered pieces of a puzzle but couldn't yet make out the big picture. The look was Code Red all the way.

He shook his head. "I don't rightly know what to make of it, but I got a bad feeling. Let me show you."

I followed him into the gym, nodding to Officers Garcia and Donaldson who guarded the door.

The middle of the court had been cordoned off with orange cones and plastic yellow tape. Something had happened inside the circle of blood. The hardwood and concrete in its center had ruptured upward, with broken boards and craggy chunks of subfloor piled around the edges of a crater. My first instinct told me a bomb had gone off—but that didn't quite fit.

"That look to you like something might have tunneled up out of the ground?" Klein asked as I stepped closer to the pit.

I hated to say it, but that's exactly how it looked. Roughly three feet in diameter, a nearly perfect round hole descended so deep into the earth it showed only blackness with no trace of an ending, and not seeing the bottom sent a chill through my bones. "What the hell could have done that?"

Klein gazed into the blackness. "Shit. Who knows. Something straight outta hell? 'Course, that leads us to the next question."

I said it for him: "Whatever it was … where did it go?"

The mobile buzzed in my pocket again. Anna's number flashed on the screen.

"Where are you?" I answered.

"Dad, people are screaming!" Her voice high-pitched and breathless. "Something's happening in the hallway! People are screaming outside our room!"

"Okay, calm down. I'm at the school. Where are you? What room?"

"Mr. Harvey's class in the East Wing. Hurry, Dad!" Panicked voices shouted in the background.

"On the way!"

Klein already had his hand on his holster.

"East wing!" I said.

He shouted for backup, as I sprinted out of the gym and raced for my little girl.

As I rounded a bend in the covered sidewalk, students and teachers exploded out of the East Wing's double doors with screams and terrified faces. I scanned the crowd, searching for Anna.

"Something's in there!" someone shouted at me. "Something *big!*"

Fighting against the tide of fleeing people, I pushed through the doors to an emptying hallway.

Something lay in the floor of the corridor about fifty feet away, where the hall made a T.

I drew my sidearm as a crowd of stragglers ran past.

The thing in the floor had a twisted shape surrounded by a reddish puddle. My every muscle tensed into a knot. It did not look human. At least, not any longer.

Lord, help me keep these kids safe.

On my left, a middle-aged face pressed against the rectangular window of a classroom door, shielding her eyes from glare. She saw me and put her hands together as if in prayer, mouthing a silent plea. I motioned her toward the exit behind me. Cautiously, she opened the door, looked both directions, then whispered for her students to make their escape. They slipped out of the classroom in speedy single file and dashed out of the building with their teacher behind them.

Klein caught up with me, gun drawn. "Garcia and Donaldson are covering the other entrance," he said, and then saw what was ahead of us. "What the hell is that?"

I approached the thing on the floor, and my first thought: a giant pile of puke.

It was worse. Twisted and bent, a skeletal human form lay sprawled in a pool of pink-red goo. The thing had no skin intact, but strips of clothing were mixed into the stew. An acrid stench hit me like a bag of sand, and I doubled over and spewed out my morning coffee. *Have mercy ...* This mangled shape was likely a student. A teenager. Alive and local and brimming with potential just this very morning. And now ... white bone shone in places through liquefied flesh.

"Anna?" I shouted down the corridor, abandoning any

pretense of standard procedure. She would always come first.
"Anna Daniels?!"

I tightened my grip on the Ruger. Its cold metal bit into my palm. The body on the floor looked like the victim of an acid bath, but I had an even more unsettling suspicion that maybe … just maybe … this poor soul had been partially digested.

Screams erupted from the classroom on my right. The door swung open and two girls leapt out. A third heavyset female tripped in the doorway, and more kids trampled right over her as she wailed and covered her head. I tried to reach for her, but the crowd was in a mad panic, shoving me backward. A woman—her teacher—tried to scoop her up. With Klein at my heels, I maneuvered past them both and charged inside. Then I froze before the ghastly thing hanging from the classroom ceiling.

Klein stuttered out some gibberish behind me, as two blue-jeaned legs wearing red Converse high-tops kicked wildly in mid-air. The lower half of the student's body dangled from a purplish mass bulging from the overhead air vent. I heard the kid's muffled screams and drew to fire … but couldn't—I'd hit the kid!

"Christ almighty!" Klein gasped at the veiny, quivering glob above us.

Those kicking legs slurped up inside some sort of orifice, and then the thing folded in on itself, and shrank back inside the vent.

"It's on the move!" I stumbled over an upturned desk and scrambled back into the hallway. The ceiling rumbled.

"Which way's it going?" Klein shouted, scanning the acoustical tiles which concealed the ductwork above us.

"Listen!"

Thumps and knocks vibrated the suspended grid. The hollow metal of the air duct moaned. With a bang, the grate of a vent ten feet away blasted off the ceiling and clanged on the linoleum floor. A purple-gray mass, fat and gelatinous, bulged out of the opening and oozed translucent slime from a hole in its center. The hole spread open and a faceless wet body slid out with a squelch and dropped to the floor in a steaming pile. It wore a pair of red Chuck Taylor high-tops, mostly dissolved but barely recognizable.

Klein and I raised our weapons and fired. We plugged the thing four or five times each, but it sucked back into the duct and disappeared again.

"Shit!" Klein shouted. He radioed Donaldson and warned them what to watch for—calling it "some kind of purple blob."

Another clamor ahead on our right. I dashed for the classroom, and my heart skipped a beat when I read the name placard: *F. Harvey.*

I threw open the door and burst inside, as the thing from the ducts slithered out of another ceiling vent. It dropped to the floor with a wet, heavy slap. Its bulbous shape, wormy but rotund like a Buick-sized maggot, pulsated within its varicose, bruise-colored skin.

The students were practically climbing the walls of the room, trying to distance themselves and make way for the exit.

"Dad!"

Anna! She cowered in the corner to my right, a book held to her chest shield-like. The terror on her face gutted me.

Klein opened fire on the creature. I did too, and we emptied both our clips, the thunder and echoes pounding my ears. Bullets plunged into the thing, but the damned beast didn't flinch, just bled black ink like it didn't matter.

But it must have had a brain, because the creature plowed ahead in the direction of the door and bulldozed eight or ten empty desks into a tangle against the entryway, sealing it off and trapping us all inside. And even half-deaf from the gunfire, I knew the screams filling the room must have shaken city hall.

The opposite wall had casement windows that would open only a few inches. One boy began bashing them with a trash can, but the shattered glass stayed in the frames.

With no better ideas, I backed up against my baby and shoved a new clip into my nine-millimeter, though I might as well have a squirt gun.

The creature reared up on one end and appeared to assess the situation. Leading with what I presumed to be its head, it slowly wormed around the room —*sniffing? searching?*—as it passed each petrified student.

As it closed in on me, my heart hammering and my finger on the trigger, I saw no eyes or nose, but the slow, methodical way it bobbed and twitched around my face suggested to me that its attacks might not be random. It was looking for someone in particular, and I prayed that Anna had never been cruel to Duke Carrington.

The creature passed by, and guilty relief flooded through me.

Along the adjacent wall, it neared a boy in a letterman jacket who had broad shoulders and big thighs. It rose up and towered above him. The other students flanking him fled to either side, as the athlete's face went white and contorted. He tried to become one with the wall behind him, clutching at the painted cinderblock. The creature loomed closer, and the kid's lips stretched to form words though no scream dared escape.

The thing drew within inches from his face. I grabbed a nearby chair in sheer desperation. Hurling it with all my strength, it bounced off the creature's back without fazing it. A circular, tooth-lined orifice opened wide in the center of its head. It spat forth a nest of writhing tongues or tentacles.

The best I could manage was: "Anna, don't watch!"

Those black tongues lashed around the boy's head like licorice whips, and he finally screamed—if only for an instant. The thing inhaled him like a hog eats a hotdog.

Anna wrapped me in her arms and buried her head between my shoulders.

Hysteria seized the students. They attacked the pile of desks that clogged the doorway, wrenching at them in a craze, or scrambling on top of them.

"Run, honey, run!" I told her.

The kids breached the entry and poured out of the classroom. She fled out the door with them. The creature appeared momentarily occupied while choking down its victim. Klein and I traded blank looks, both dumbstruck about what to do next. If we shoot it, we hit the kid inside— even though the kid was likely dead.

"We need heavy artillery," Klein said in a deadpan. He bolted out of the room.

So did I, only to find Anna waiting for me in the corridor. "I told you to get out of here!"

"I won't leave you!"

The creature suddenly squeezed through the doorway and flopped onto the hallway floor. One of its ends lifted up and swiveled in our direction.

"Damn it, run!" I hollered. "Run, Anna, run!"

With a lunge and a stretch, it bounded after us. We sprinted like hell. And, God forgive me, I fired as I ran. I lost my senses, and I pulled the trigger blindly behind me, trying to slow it so Anna could get away.

Ahead of me, she banged out of the hallway doors onto the sidewalk. The monster stayed right on my heels. "Faster! Keep going!"

She kept running down the sidewalk as I flew through the doorway behind her. The thing slowed as it pushed through the doors, but then it came barreling right after us again. The students and teachers outside scattered in every direction.

We were heading back the way I'd come, toward the gymnasium.

I had an idea: "Anna, take a left. Get off the sidewalk!"

To our right, the wall of the north wing enclosed a small courtyard, but to the left she could make a break for the baseball fields. And that's the direction she raced.

I glanced back as the thing charged at me with a burst of speed. The sidewalk veered right, so I lunged to my left in a flying leap. The thing's flank glanced my shoe as it passed. I stumbled on the landing but regained balance and ran toward Anna, who was still putting distance between herself and danger.

The creature diverted its course from us. Or rather, we'd simply been in the way. Gathering my wits, I headed back after it.

Principal Phillips saw it coming first. Standing in front of the gym's entryway with two officers, her eyes grew tenfold and she slapped her hands over her heart. The screech she let out shattered her strictly-business demeanor. The officers drew their useless sidearms and staggered backward.

"Move!" I shouted at them as I chased it. "Get out of the way!"

And they must have heard me, because they all scampered away.

The big maggot slowed in front of the gym doors and wallowed to a stop. It made a turn and squeezed through the doors back toward its point of origin.

Just then, Klein rushed up wearing a backpack-mounted tank and a handheld flame thrower—a donation to the department from the local VFW, who probably hadn't expected us to restore it to working condition.

I raised my gun mostly out of habit, and we both charged inside. Finding no sign of noise or beast, we approached the hole in the floor. In a soupy pool roughly ten feet away from it, another ruined body lay splayed across the basketball court. Shreds of the kid's letterman jacket remained barely intact—just enough for me to read the name stitched across the shoulders: *Quimby*.

I felt sick. I mean, what are the odds?

Cones and police tape lay scattered. From the slimy puddle, a broad red smear led down into the pit. The creature must have slithered back to wherever it had come from.

"Goddamn it," Klein muttered, ready to barbecue the thing.

"It's gone," I said. "Maybe it's over."

We walked closer to the hole and peered inside. No longer bottomless, the tunnel ended some six feet down, clogged with dirt and rock.

The whole ordeal defied logical explanation … but then again, this was Trapper Valley.

I walked outside to look for my daughter. To hug her.

But as I stepped onto the sidewalk, I felt eyes on me. A nagging suspicion. We had a visitor. I glassed the campus with a keen eye on the background scenery, looking for remote areas suited for a secret spectator. I scoured the baseball fields, the nearest parking lot, the roofs of the educational buildings. And I found him.

"There," I said, pointing.

Klein, now at my side, followed my gaze.

On a grassy hilltop alongside the bleachers of the football stadium some hundred yards away, a single lanky figure stood looking through a pair of binoculars. I knew without a doubt this was Duke Carrington, watching from a safe distance as his grand plan unleashed its carnage on everyone else. He quickly lowered the binoculars and jogged away.

I went for the car.

"Ritch, what are you doing?" Klein said from behind me.

I paid no attention, slammed the door, started the cruiser.

"Ritch, no! Wait on me!"

I was gone, the tires squealing as I swerved out of the lot and bee-lined it to the delivery route that swept up behind the stadium. That cowardly little shit had just killed at least three people, probably more. And he had to pay.

A siren wailed as Klein pulled up behind me in his Bronco. I had no plans to stop. I tore through the open gate of a chain-link fence and sped onto the blacktop that ran uphill behind the bleachers. As I reached the peak, I caught sight of Carrington scaling the fence down below. *Damn!*

I cut a sharp turn and left the road, rambling down the grassy hillside toward the fence. The car quaked and bounced, and my neck and spine rattled. With a punch of the brakes, the cruiser jerked to a stop. I popped out of the car and scaled the fence in no time, fueled by pure adrenaline.

The kid was really hoofing it, but I was a man possessed and gained on him fast. When he slowed to look back, my shoulder met his and sent him hurtling onto the ground.

"Fucking murderer!" I ripped him from the asphalt and flipped him over, straddling his torso to pin him down. He stared at me with wild, red-circled eyes as he gasped for breath. A tear hit his cheek. One of my tears. I drew back my fist to shatter his face. "You piece of shit!"

"Stop it!" shouted Klein from over my shoulder.

"This bastard just killed a bunch of kids," I said. "*Kids!*"

"He's a kid, too!"

"I don't care!" I tightened my knuckles.

"Don't do it, Ritch!"

I'd be screwed if I hit a minor, and this kid knew it. I saw it in his face.

"It's a Code Black!" Klein said. "Ritch … it's a Code Black."

I froze when he said it. Locking eyes with Duke Carrington made me want to kill him more than ever. Because I saw smugness in the kid's eyes. As I stared at him, I saw a sense of victory somewhere deep inside those red circles. The hint of a smile twitched at the corners of his mouth. Revenge was his, he thought. This little shit thought he'd gotten away with murder. After all, a monster did it, and who could possibly prove in a court of law, beyond a reasonable doubt, that this teenager was responsible for the monster?

Klein was right. A situation like this called for a Code Black.

I unclenched my fist.

***

The next week, I attended three of Trapper Valley's four closed-coffin funerals. We'd found the fourth body in the boys' restroom. I did not attend the service of Greg Quimby, son of Clay Quimby, because I already had enough to bear, and I could only be so magnanimous when in bitter spirits.

Or maybe I just didn't want to see anymore.

On the following Saturday night, Officer Garcia booked Vince Carrington for a DUI, locking him in a cage next to his father, who was already being held for putting Mercy in the hospital with three fresh broken ribs.

It must be hell living in a place like that… But my heart grew hard, once a sympathetic fella like Duke Carrington linked arms with the devil. Cold-blooded murder crossed the line of forgiveness. That's when I quit caring about how a body turned out to be evil, and focused only on how to stop the evil. That's why I became a lawman: The pursuit of justice.

But sometimes the law does not achieve justice. Sometimes there's a loophole, like in Trapper Valley, where every once in a while, some nefarious individual exacts a kind of evil that's not covered in law books or police training, or hell, even in a science class. Some situations defied the natural order of things, and transcended the constructs of men who meant well but didn't have all the answers. In those rare situations, justice had to be carried out beyond the reach of the law, because the law just didn't have enough reach. That's when we call a Code Black.

'Night, Dad. Love you!

The message from Anna felt like a warm breeze through the chilly evening. She always texted me goodnight when I pulled the late shift. I was sitting in my cruiser in the shadows of a parking lot alongside the darkened Trapper Valley Church of Christ, clocking speeders. But not really.

I was waiting.

Soon, I heard a rumble in the distance. I clicked the ignition over to the utility setting and quietly inched down the window. Approaching from my left, the yellow glare of headlamps lit the way for a growling diesel engine. A tinkling noise accompanied the vehicle, and I could tell from its racket and the shape of the lights that the pickup belonged to Earl Ketchum, who ran a local mechanic's shop. It was his work truck. A good bet would place pawn-shop owner Sonny Wallace in the passenger seat. They'd been deputized, so to speak, although completely off the books.

The pickup was dragging something from the back, bathed in the red glow of the taillights. A shudder ran through me when I realized Duke Carrington, wrapped in rope and gagged with duct tape, was skidding down the road tethered to a tow chain. Sparks leapt like fiery crickets as the metal links skittered over the blacktop. Beneath it, I heard the muffled squeals of the kid as the gritty asphalt sanded off his hide. At this rate, he'd be nearly skinless in a matter of minutes, just like the victims of the beast he'd summoned with that damned hill magic… A sentence a bit too gruesome for my taste, but I suppose it had a certain poetry to it.

It was Code Black all the way.

And I never saw a thing.

The End

Vampire Lake

The locals called it Vampire Lake because they had no real imagination. That accursed black water pooled against a 70-year-old concrete dam deep within the woods of Shady Brake, Alabama. The lake had been forgotten by most, other than the occasional kayaker and teenagers on ATVs. Nobody ever swam in the water. Some folks claimed it had been contaminated by the old chemical plant that once occupied the property. Others claimed the lake had been tainted by something far more sinister.

My best friend Gilby Peters had a different outlook entirely.

"Let's go swimming this weekend," Gilby muttered under his breath. He sat next to me during fourth-period biology.

"Go swimming where?" I asked in a whisper. This was October of '93, and all the pools had closed weeks ago.

"Vampire Lake."

I gave him a look. He raised an eyebrow at me.

"Dude," I said. "Supposed to be bad water. You know that. Parasites and disease and stuff."

He looked up at the ceiling, as if maybe God were up there giving him a shrug, then he looked back at me.

"You ever heard of anyone getting a disease from the water?" When Gilby set his mind on something, there was no turning back. I could see where this was heading.

"No," I said. "But I've never known anyone to swim in it, either, because it's known to be *contaminated*."

"Mr. Kerrick…" interrupted our teacher Mrs. Hallman with the horse-like teeth. "Is there something you'd like to share with the rest of the class?"

Why do teachers say things like that? Had I wanted to share something with the class, I'd have raised my hand or even sang it out loud while standing on her desk. I sure wouldn't whisper it to Gilby.

"No, ma'am."

Gilby and I both rolled our eyes.

Saturday afternoon, we went to Vampire Lake.

***

They say if you don't like the weather in Alabama, wait twenty minutes and it'll change. The leaves had dried and fallen after a long, hot summer, and the ground was a crunchy carpet of red, gold and brown. Friday had been hot and muggy, but Saturday was gray with clouds, and the air had the early chill of winter. Diving into cold water sounded like torture to me. I'd only come along for the boat ride.

Gilby, on the other hand, kept charging full steam ahead with his big idea, and had even convinced his airhead girlfriend Debbie that a trip to Vampire Lake was something she couldn't miss. She wore ruby lipstick, a big blonde bouffant, tiny jean shorts, and a skin-tight Rolling Stones shirt that showed a big red tongue lolling out a mouth. I didn't care much for Debbie, but she showed up with a cooler of beer, so I kept my complaints to myself.

We hauled the row-boat beneath a bridge along Grayson Drive. We had to wade down the creek with the flat-bottom carried between us until the water got deep enough for us to pile in and paddle. Debbie carried the cooler—no easy feat for a tiny girl made mostly of tits and hair.

Smooth sailing from there to the lake, and along the way we laughed and drank, and told jokes, and drank. Gilby kept trying to grab handfuls of Debbie, and she kept swatting him away, complaining that I could see what they were doing.

"You're being naughty, Gilby!" she'd squeal and giggle.

I felt like a huge fifth wheel but tried not to pay attention, just laughed and rowed and drank heavier.

No vampires in sight, by the way. The lake, though, had a strange darkness to it. The inkiness had to be due to something in the water rather than its depth, and speculating about whatever gave the lake its eerie blackness did stir the imagination. No wonder the place got such a bad rap with the vampires and what-not.

I was hammered by the time we rounded a bend and that big, gray dam came into view. It barricaded the lake about 50 feet wide.

A few fallen trees had died in the water to the left of the dam, with their black, bony branches blocking the way ashore. We paddled for the right side of the bank, where I hopped over the bow and dragged the boat through mud so deep it swallowed my sneakers—not an easy chore while shitfaced on Budweiser.

Once ashore, Gilby and Debbie busied themselves with molesting each other, which gave me time to blaze a big, fat joint I'd been saving. Happy to give my rowing shoulders a rest, I dropped onto my butt, leaned against a tree, and sparked up.

***

Mary Jane and I were getting along famously. White Zombie's "Black Sunshine" blared through my Walkman, while I puffed and puffed and puffed. I was drifting away into a doobie-land nap, when I heard a scream and a splash that cut through Jay Yuenger's wailing guitar.

Gilby and Debbie had ventured onto the dam, which I figured to be about five feet wide. Seems like halfway across, he thought it'd be cute to shove her into the lake. She plunged in with a gnarly splash.

Gilby nearly lost his balance, pinwheeling his arms so as not to tip over and fall off the steep side of the dam—a good 30-foot drop.

Just as he steadied himself, Debbie exploded up from the water. Gilby yelped as she grabbed his ankles. She snatched his feet off the dam and pitched herself backward, sinking down again and bringing Gilby with her.

"Shit!" he hollered, as he slid into the black, the concrete ledge raking his back on the way down. They both disappeared beneath the surface.

***

I thought they'd never come up.

I ripped off my headphones and stood on the bank trying to see something—anything—in the pitch-black depths, but it was impossible.

And when they finally emerged, they were different.

I fully admit to being three sheets to the wind, but I saw what I saw.

"Why'd you throw me in? You fucking piece of shit!" Debbie snarled at Gilby after coughing up the creek water. I had never heard her swear. She waded ashore wiping black mud and gunk from her face.

A slime-covered Gilby trudged out of the water behind her. "'Cause you deserved it, whore." He spoke in a voice as flat and unfeeling as an eviction notice. "You shoulda drowned down there."

Now, I knew Gilby as a perpetual jokester, but he didn't sound as though he were joking. He sounded nothing like the friend I knew.

"Not before I cut you open and pull out all your insides," she told him.

To say the least, the mood had changed.

Both of them stood glaring at each other on the edge of the bank, covered from head to toe in some sort of tar-like substance that seemed like it should have rinsed off in the water.

"Try it, cunt," Gilby dared her. "Give it a shot, and watch me break your head open and eat everything that falls out."

I could not believe my ears. Something had gone very wrong. And all the splashing had stirred up a stink that made me gag—a smell of rot and shit and dead things.

The shore laid scattered with dead branches and debris, and Debbie bent down and picked up a four-foot tree limb with one end broken into a point.

Gilby grumbled something at her that I couldn't quite understand because it came out in a kind of ragged growl.

I'm not sure what possessed Gilby to rush at Debbie. To attack her? To disarm her? He never got the chance, though, because she disarmed *him*.

She thrust that big stick at him. He threw up a forearm to block it. The spear tip sheared right through the muscle and ripped a deep gash from his wrist to his elbow. The meat of his arm opened up in a flap.

Gilby moaned at the sight of all the blood, and Debbie again raised her makeshift spear.

Horrified, I backed away by pure instinct.

Gilby looked at me then at Debbie and must've seen the same murder in her eyes as I did. But instead of shrinking in fear, he clenched his good fist and roared, "You bitch!"

He charged at her. Too slow, though.

She lunged and stabbed the tree branch right into his eye. With a squelch, it sank deep into his face.

My blood ran cold. I froze where I stood.

Gilby's legs buckled. He collapsed to his knees. Debbie planted a muddy foot on his right shoulder and ripped the stick out of his skull. He fell over and twitched on the ground.

The whole world seemed to go still and silent. Then she turned to me.

I dashed for the rowboat.

Luck placed me nearer to it than her, if only by 12 feet or so. With a sprint and a leap, I rolled into the boat, snatched up an oar, and pushed the hull off the bank as Debbie splashed into the water—a total blackened maniac.

She chased me like a demon, tearing through the water and growling like a rabid animal. Her speed was stunning. I paddled like hell but glanced back to see her climbing over the stern.

I thought of diving into the lake, but one look at that black water stopped me.

Glassing the woods around me, I screamed, "Help! Somebody help me!" but the place was deserted. Nothing around but looming trees, craggy branches, dark shadows and murky depths.

Her nails ripped the flesh of my back. Her fingers slid around my neck. She roared and climbed onto my shoulders, tearing at my left eye. I'd never seen such fury from a human. I dropped the oar and wrenched at her, but *good god* her strength! I couldn't shake her. She bit my face like a mad dog, chomping and tearing. I heard my skin grind between her teeth. My ear fell to the floor of the boat. *Bitch is eating me alive!*

I threw myself backward, crashing onto her and pinning her against a wooden seat. That knocked her off me. In that instant, I grabbed an oar, spun around and whipped it over my shoulder. She bolted upright, but I brought the paddle down to crush her feral face. Bone crunched on impact, and she fell back. In a rage, I smashed her again, and the oar's edge sunk between her eyes and split her mud-caked head. I kept bringing the paddle down, over and over, telling myself this thing was not Debbie! Because Debbie was gone! She was somewhere down below! *This thing could not be Debbie!*

She finally went still and died with no stake in her heart.

***

No vampires exist in Vampire Lake, but something else does. Something much worse lurks in that water. It's something that I can never forget nor hide from. I'm reminded every time I look in the mirror to apply my prosthetic nose, or insert my glass eye, or brush my hair in a particular way that conceals my missing ear.

I still miss ol' Gilby. And even poor, poor Debbie.

Damn that terrible place.

The End

Bad Brunch in the Big Easy

Marty Fetzer beamed at his new wife over the brunch menu outside a corner café in New Orleans. "What looks good to you, dear?"

"You do." Lydia blew him a kiss. Marty puckered up and caught it. They sat at a wrought-iron patio table, watching the French Quarter tourists bustle about the sidewalk, while enjoying the lively jazz music from a trio of street performers half a block away.

Marty, bald and fat with a nasty case of psoriasis, would be the first to admit that Lydia Tyler was way out of his league. How he'd convinced such a vision of beauty to take his hand in marriage posed nearly as much a mystery to him as everyone else in his small circle of friends. He figured his money probably helped. Nevertheless, he resolved to enjoy the experience while it lasted because he was certain of one irrefutable fact: One day his luck would run out.

"A lot to choose from," he said, reviewing all the rich breakfast dishes laced with spicy Cajun flair; scrambled eggs with alligator sausage, creole shrimp and grits with cheesy hash-browns.

"It's so hard to decide," Lydia said with a tinge of excitement. "Everything looks so delicious." She lifted her eyes to him, two shining pools of still blue water, ever enchanting Marty with her delicate features and the small mole at the corner of her mouth. "Maybe I'll have the eggs benedict. Or a mushroom-and-cheese omelet."

She could eat like a teenage boy yet always keep her slender figure—just one of many things that made his wife so special.

"Sounds tasty," he said. "You should order both, and top it all off with some whipped cream and chocolate syrup."

She tossed her auburn curls and wrinkled her nose. "You're silly."

"You're beautiful."

Her eyes brightened. "And you're brilliant."

Marty blushed, knowing if anyone were to overhear these exchanges they'd probably gag, but he didn't care. After all, this was their honeymoon.

He'd told her countless times that no, he was far from brilliant, only lucky enough to land the easy job of dropping catchy phrases into his publisher's preconceived plotline. But Lydia wouldn't hear of it. She gushed over his eloquent word choice and romantic characterization, citing it as undeniable proof that he had the soul of an artist and the heart of a selfless lover.

Clasping one of his books to her chest, she'd say something like: "*After the rescue at Criswell Manor, when Alexander Devereux buries his face in the spun honey of Lady Jessica's hair, and kisses her soft, warm rose-petal skin while professing his devotion with such passion it pains him—that's you and I, Marty. I can feel our love in your words.*"

Marty always fought the urge to roll his eyes when she said such things. Was there truly a quality to his writing that had more promise than a paycheck?

Marty finally accepted the idea. Inner beauty must actually exist, and he made peace with the idea that Lydia found it within him. This was yet another admirable strength of her character, because he doubted he could ever fall in love with someone as unattractive as himself.

One night after a walk in the park, he proposed to her beneath a summer moon. They married two months later.

"So, how do you like New Orleans?" she asked.

"Charming." Marty took a drink of his bloody mary. "The food's fantastic. The music, the history, the culture. Very unique."

Truthfully, Marty thought the streets smelled like urine and the nightlife was teeming with drunken idiots. But he had to admit that from its rakish women and historical brothels to its weird voodoo traditions, New Orleans did have a certain seedy charm.

"I knew you'd feel that way. It's one of my all-time favorite cities." Lydia took a piece of French bread from the basket between them and dipped it into a saucer of olive oil. "There's no place like it on earth."

Marty's skin itched, and he scratched his side. Still pudgy, he'd lost almost twenty pounds for the wedding and was leaning begrudgingly toward the fruit bowl with a side of cottage cheese, when he heard the wail of police sirens.

The sound of skidding tires screeched around the street corner. He looked up to see a yellow car slide sideways through the intersection. Horns blaring, two oncoming vehicles swerved to miss it. A dodging truck smacked into a lamppost across the street.

"My god!" Lydia gasped.

Momentum shot the yellow hatchback across the intersection. Its rear end fanned around as it made a fish-tailing U-turn, smoke billowing from its tires. Two pursuing cop cruisers slammed their brakes, one rear-ending the other. The yellow car now careened toward the street alongside the café. Its front tire blew with a shotgun bang, and the bumper dropped down, the car grinding across the cobblestones in Lydia's direction.

Marty swept the table over and lunged at her, snatching his wife and diving. With Lydia wrapped in his arms, he twisted to absorb the impact as they crashed onto the pavement.

An explosion of metal and glass showered them with debris as the car ripped through the patio. Marty rolled, cradling Lydia's head, and kept tumbling away from the chaos until his back slammed into the café wall.

Cries and screams surrounded them.

"You okay?! Honey, are you all right?"

"Yes," Lydia said from the crook of his neck. She looked up at him. Her eyes, wide with alarm, relaxed a degree, and a soft smile touched her lips. Marty read it as her sense of security. "Yes. I'm fine. Thanks to you."

In that brief moment his pride swelled, and he felt a warmth in his heart.

Then he became conscious of the melee around them. The vehicle had slammed into the café wall and partially through the stucco-covered cinderblock. The driver's door hung wide open with no one inside. Its dashboard radio blasted the static squeal of a lost signal. Pinned beneath the car, two thin legs wearing high heels stuck out from the undercarriage.

Marty's back ached. His elbows bled. He let go of Lydia and slowly climbed an overturned chair to steady his legs.

A man with long black hair struggled with two waiters, shoving one thin boy to the ground and clawing at the face of the other. Marty guessed him to be the driver—a crazed person who snorted and growled like an animal.

An elderly woman with an open wound on her head limped across the patio. The snarling man grabbed her by the arms and hurled her into the tangle of upturned furniture. He tore his way across the clutter, heading for the street and Lydia, who knelt in his way, dusting herself off.

Marty stared at the man's eyes, dark red like two gory plums without a fleck of white, surely a sign of insanity. Marty's pulse galloped. He clenched his teeth and charged at the madman. But his shin struck a hard object, and his legs buckled. He spilled forward, landing on the hard points of scattered tables and chairs.

Lydia howled in terror. Marty flipped over to see the man looming above his wife, her throat in his clutches. With her mouth gaping wide, fighting for air, the man pulled her close and vomited in her face. A flood of blackish foulness poured over her.

Marty moaned and floundered off the pile of metal. Scrambling to his feet, he grabbed a chair, lifted it high and whirled around to club the maniac. A police officer seized it from him as two other cops jerked the man off Lydia and shoved him into a wall. Then they threw the bastard face-down to the ground while they cuffed him.

Lydia hit her knees heaving and puking out the vile inky sickness. Marty's vision blurred with tears. The cop released him. He stumbled over and threw his arms around her. He grabbed a cloth napkin from a fallen table to help clean her off.

"I'm so sorry," he said. "Baby, I'm sorry." Her body shook beneath him.

Blue and red lights swirled around the wreckage as emergency vehicles roared onto the scene. The madman on the ground squirmed and kicked, gnashing his teeth with beastlike grunts. Marty closed his eyes and hugged his wife as she buried her face in his shoulder and trembled with deep, heavy sobs.

***

She caught whatever that bastard had.

Marty's dashboard GPS led him alongside one of the vast iron-fenced New Orleans graveyards, populated with row after row of above-ground crypts adorned with gothic artistry carved of granite or marble. Angels. Sculptures of the Virgin Mary. Gargoyles. Gray and white buildings, full of history and human rot, flashed past the car window, luring tourists from all over to marvel at the morbid décor.

Before the incident at the café, Lydia had told him a couple of conflicting theories to explain why the tombs had been built above ground. By far the most gruesome was the theory of the city's percolation problems. Since New Orleans lay below sea level, the water table was extremely high. Burying the dead could feasibly result in floating corpses bubbling up from beneath the ground all the way to the surface during a heavy flood.

Marty's skin prickled with gooseflesh as he pictured a river of rotten bodies flowing down the city sidewalk—just one more ghoulish reason to hate this damned city.

A robotic female voice from the console alerted him to an approaching turn. He'd soon arrive at his destination and hopefully find some help for his ailing wife.

The white wood-sided house, with peeling paint and a sagging porch, had been divided into a shotgun double. Marty parked on the curb and rang the bell of the door on the left.

"Hello," he said to the woman with candied-apple hair who opened a crack in the doorway. "Are you Ms. Charlotte Haverty?"

"Charla. Maybe. Who are you?"

"My name is Martin Fetzer. I found your name in the newspaper. Your husband's obituary."

Her eyes fell away. The incident at the café, and what happened afterward, had made the local headlines. According to reports, the crazed driver of the yellow car, Darren Haverty, had broken free of his restraints during transport to the hospital psychiatry ward. After strangling a paramedic to death and stabbing another, he stole an ambulance and led the police on another lengthy chase. Once cornered, he resisted arrest. The cops shot him fourteen times.

"I don't know you," she said.

"I don't mean to be a bother, ma'am. But I was there that day. At the café. My wife was there, too."

She glanced to either side of him, as if looking for a camera crew. "The café? You saw Darren?"

"Yes, ma'am. That's what I wanted to talk to you about."

After a moment she took a step back and shut the door. Marty worried that was to be the end of it, and then heard the jingle of the chain-link unlocking. The door reopened wide. Charla Haverty had a short pixie haircut and a long black nightgown that painted her slender thighs and floated just above her bare feet.

"Did you know my husband?" she asked. "I don't remember meeting you."

"Never seen him before that morning, ma'am."

Charla brushed her bangs aside and stepped onto the porch. "Then how can I help you?"

"He was sick, your husband. He was infected with some kind of disease. Am I right?"

She tensed slightly and frowned. "No." One hand held a glass of red wine, which she lifted and sipped with gleaming cherry lips. "You're *not* right."

"But I saw him slobbering with bloodshot eyes, babbling like he'd lost his mind."

"Why do you ask, Mr..."

"Fetzer," Marty reminded her. "Because my wife's sick."

"I'm sorry about that. But what does that have to do with Darren?"

Marty sighed through his nose. He did not want to go into details. This poor woman had just endured a great loss, and as maniacal as the man may have been, Marty could take no joy in casting her dead husband in an unflattering light.

"I have reason to believe that he may have infected my wife with whatever illness was ailing him. I need to know what kind of virus or bacteria or whatever that I'm dealing with. That *she's* now dealing with."

"Darren didn't have a virus." She tilted her head, the shape of an inverted teardrop but with a soft, delicate chin. "Have you taken her to a doctor? That seems like it would be the first step."

Of course a trip to the doc had been his first reaction, even before Lydia had shown signs that she was ... *off*.

"She won't go," Marty said. "She refuses. I can't talk any sense into her."

Charla lifted the glass to her lips and took a drink. She leaned back, and her glare softened. "What are her symptoms?"

Marty explained that Lydia's entire personality seemed to pivot on that ghastly encounter with Charla's husband. Lydia hadn't looked at him the same since the initial shock of it all. He blamed his failure to protect her, and felt utterly unworthy in her presence. Nevertheless, he thought the effect would wear off.

But it hadn't. In fact, the situation had worsened.

"We just married a week ago," he said. "I swear that until that very moment at the café, we couldn't keep our hands off each other. One minute we're having an amazing honeymoon, and then—*the incident*—and she's another person."

Charla held his gaze with an almost imperceptible nod of the head.

"At first, all she would do is stare at the TV or out the window," Marty said. "This is a woman with an irrepressible zest for life, but now ... *nothing*. She's like a blank canvas. And the more I try to engage her, to comfort her, to show her affection or just simply have a conversation with her ... that's when she gets mean."

Yesterday he'd tried to be firm. He unplugged the television, seized Lydia by the arm and demanded she accompany him outside for a walk. She needed fresh air. Staying cooped up in the rental bungalow was a waste of a vacation and detrimental to her mental health. *I'm not going anywhere!* she'd snarled at him and reared back a hand as though she meant to claw off his face. He retreated and never gave her the chance. She went back to her TV.

"This is out of character? Her being so temperamental?" Charla said.

"Absolutely. And today she's acting downright vicious, like I'm not her husband but her arch enemy."

Charla looked into the distance for a moment, then down at the ground. "Does she hit you? Or break things?"

Marty got the inkling that Charla had witnessed her husband's violent impulses before his fateful trip in the yellow car. It weighted her emerald eyes with dark circles and pulled at her pouting lip. He wanted to hug her. And the way her dress clung to her curves, he wanted to be hugged by her.

Marty stifled the thought and refocused on his wife. "That's what worries me. The way Lydia's condition is progressing ... I worry about what's coming next."

Charla nodded and pursed her lips. "You *should* worry."

"You know something, don't you? What's happening to her? What am I supposed to do?"

Charla finished her wine and wiped her lips with a stroke of two well-manicured fingers painted with ruby nail polish. "I don't know much. Honestly. Darren was sort of ... *eclectic*. He was an artist and a musician, kind of a heavy-metal hipster. Creative and curious, always dabbling in this or that belief system, be it Wicca or some other pagan mysticism — the stranger the better, as far as he was concerned. He didn't believe in any of those things, but he *wanted* to believe. He was always searching for the truth in advertising, if you know what I mean. Trying to find that one true religion. But with Darren, seeing was believing, and he wanted to *see* God. *Any* god. An angel or a demon — didn't matter to him. Anything that gave him proof that another world existed."

She adjusted her gown, the wide collar of which had been slinking south of her cleavage.

"Anyway, once we got settled, Darren became intrigued by some of the local voodoo customs. He made some friends. They were into weird shit." She shrugged. "And now he's dead."

"What kind of weird shit?"

"I wasn't privy to the details. He became very secretive before he fell apart that day. Maybe he thought he was protecting me. I didn't pay much attention at the time. But lately he'd become convinced that he was closing in on the truth that he'd always been searching for. He told me that much."

"And you think his sickness was somehow associated with his interest in ... what — voodoo?"

"Or maybe hoodoo. There's a difference, you know. I don't know what it is, but Darren could've told you. You want to know more, then go talk to Jean-Louis Dubois. That's the sonofabitch he was running with."

Marty pulled a pen from his pocket and wrote the name on his palm.

"He owns a voodoo shop in the Quarter. It's in the phone book. He was giving Darren a crash course in practices and beliefs. I figured it was a waste of money. But now I think I was wrong. There's something to it, and Darren got too close. Maybe he'd still be alive if he had just stayed away from it all. Anyway, I think Dubois had something to do with what happened."

Marty processed this information and realized he had found a "lead," just like a detective in a crime novel. In spite of his heavy heart, he felt a faint spark of excitement. After years in the by-the-numbers romance game, he was finally working on a new plot.

***

Marty entered the rental flat with plastic bags in each hand. The lights were out. The kitchen faucet was running at full blast. The television, tuned to a channel with no service, broadcast only a swirl of black-and-white distortion that hissed with static.

Lydia sat with her legs folded in the recliner at the center of the darkened living room, staring at the TV and stroking something in her lap.

"I brought groceries," Marty said.

Lydia did not acknowledge his presence. He walked to the kitchen counter and set down the bags, withdrawing a half gallon of milk, a block of cheddar and a bread loaf, all of which he shelved in the fridge.

His wife's wedding and engagement rings lay in a shell-shaped soap dish near the kitchen sink. He scooped them up and stuck them in his pocket. He then shut off the faucet, and noticed Lydia twitch when he did. With the running water now silent, she slid to the edge of the seat and stared even more intently into the buzzing TV screen, as if drawn to the noise.

He stepped around to face her and saw the new pet.

"Where'd you get the cat?" he asked. A scruffy gray and white feline lay curled between her folded legs, and she caressed behind its ears as it purred comfortably.

Lydia said nothing, only stared into the white noise.

"You plan on adopting a stray?" Over the last couple of days, he'd noticed a half dozen of them lingering around the sidewalk outside the rental.

Lydia's eyes had sunk into dark shallows, her cheeks looked hollow, and her hair hadn't been brushed in three days. Marty still found her beautiful.

"I want you to know I'm working on this. I have an idea who might be able to help you. I'm going to get you well."

She gave no sign that she heard or saw him. He walked to the TV and turned it off, then returned to his wife and kneeled in front of her.

"Lydia, if you can hear me, I want you to know that I love you. And I'm determined to make you well."

"Turn it back on," she said.

"Honey, you're watching too much TV. There wasn't even a program playing."

"Turn it back on," she growled. Her fingernails dug into her thigh as she spoke. "I want it on, now."

His face grew hot with anger. Enough was enough, and he felt sick of being ignored. "No," he said. "I'm going out. I have some things to take care of. I'll be back later. You want the tube on, then turn it on yourself."

Marty stomped across the room and swung open the front door. Lydia's voice rose from a snarl to a shriek as she screamed at his back *"Daaamn youuu, youuuu baaassstaaard!"*

He slammed the door behind him, and a chill coursed through his spine when, mingled with her scream, came the yowling warble of a cat in agony, a prolonged groan that sputtered and choked.

Marty clutched himself around the shoulders. *Good God, what was she doing to the poor thing?*

Something thumped hard against the door and slid down onto the floor inside.

Marty ran to his Volvo and scrambled inside. He started the car, and the oldies station blared out soul music. He slapped the radio until it went off and then he tore down the street. Lydia was losing her mind, or had lost it already, and Marty had the sinking feeling that he hadn't much time to set things right.

***

Jean-Louis Dubois's lamp-lit shop, just a skip off Canal Road, smelled of smoke and pungent herbs. Shelves full of books, hand-sewn dolls and bottled powders adorned the walls. Small, colorful bags labeled "gris gris" filled two display cases, and hundreds of decorated candles cluttered two more. Voodoo practitioners apparently also had a need for copper pennies, coffin nails, lobster claws and chicken feet.

"Ms. Haverty sent you?" Dubois said through grinning yellow teeth that shined through the low light and his dark skin. "Strange that she would do that, as I didn't think she cared for me very much."

"She said you might be able to give me answers about my wife. Her name is Lydia. She now seems to be suffering from the same affliction as Darren Haverty."

Dubois's lips slid over his teeth, and the smile disappeared. "How could that be? Was she acquainted with Mr. Haverty?"

"No. She was attacked by Haverty at the café where he crashed his car. He threw up in her face. The most disgusting thing I've ever seen. Now she looks deathly sick, won't listen to a word I say, and she seems to be slipping away, mentally."

"I assume you've consulted a doctor."

Marty rubbed his forehead, exasperated. "She refuses. Look, if you've got any idea what I'm dealing with, I'd greatly appreciate your insight. I'm at my—"

"Do you believe in the spirit world, Mr. Fetzer?" The dreadlocked Dubois, with his beige robe and strange symbols hanging from his many necklaces, raised an eyebrow and fixed on Marty. The burning incense on his desk produced a serpentine curl of smoke that floated in the air beside him.

"I don't know. Maybe," Marty said. "I was raised Catholic. I suppose I'm not very devout, but I like to keep an open mind."

"Ah," Dubois said with a nod. "An open mind. That can be a fine approach to new experiences, but an open mind can also be an open door. It's wise to know when to shut it, lest something wander inside that you don't want to meet."

"Is that what happened to Haverty? Something wandered inside?"

"Wandered in..." Dubois said. "You might say he rolled out the red carpet."

"And you helped him do it?"

Dubois gave a voiceless laugh, a ticking sound from deep in his throat. "No, my friend. I sell books and charms. I introduced him to some informational resources, which I now regret doing, but Mr. Haverty acted of his own free will—and against my warnings. You see, I am a spiritual individual. I have faith. Mr. Haverty, however, had no faith. To believe in the spirits, he felt he had to see the other side first-hand."

"What did he see?"

"He saw, Mr. Fetzer, exactly what he called forth."

"Which was..." Marty persisted, growing agitated with Dubois's evasive mumbo-jumbo.

"If God were to appear to every man who demanded to see proof, there would be no need for blind faith. It is through faith that God reigns. God does not bend to the arrogant demands of man."

"What are you saying?"

"I'm saying that demons are another matter altogether. Demons lurk in the borderlands, licking their lips at the prospect of attaining a vessel. Demons are all too eager to appear to men who call, because if a man gets too close, the demon can exert its influence. The demon takes control. The demon then has a power it would not otherwise have, and it becomes closer to a god. And may the Lord have mercy on anyone foolish or unfortunate enough to fall under the thing's influence."

"The Lord didn't have much mercy on Darren Haverty," Marty said. "Are you trying to tell me that he infected my wife with some sort of ... *demon?* That she's *possessed?*"

A customer came into the store, jingling a tiny bell above the door which distracted Dubois. He turned back to Marty. "I don't know that to be the case. And I don't know it *not* to be the case, Mr. Fetzer. I do not have all the answers. But I do know what Haverty was seeking. It sounds like he may have found it. And, sadly, he may have shared it with your wife."

Marty's skin suddenly itched all over, and he felt uncomfortably hot. What he was hearing made no rational sense, yet the way Lydia was acting simply *was not* rational.

"My God," Marty said. "Is there anything I can do to save her?"

Dubois tilted his head and stroked his chin. "Perhaps."

***

Night fell on New Orleans.

Marty parked the car in the bungalow driveway. His heart pounded. His moment of last resort had arrived.

He gathered up the supply bags from the passenger seat, trying to ignore the nagging suspicion that Jean-Louis Dubois was nothing but a liar who'd just swindled him out of two-hundred bucks for an armload of useless voodoo gimmicks. The man's instructions had sounded like something from a J.K. Rowling fantasy, but Marty found himself with precious few options—the most painful being the prospect of Lydia's forced committal to a psychiatric hospital. The ultimate white flag of surrender. And if what Dubois said about her affliction proved true, then even that would be a pointless endeavor.

Marty was sure of only one thing: The clock was ticking.

He unlocked the front door. The dank smell of sweat and soiled clothing hung thickly in the air of the darkened suite. The sizzle of television static meshed with the hiss of running water from the kitchen and the bathroom faucets. Smeared across the floor at the foot of the door was a crusting red stain, but Marty saw no cat carcass.

Lydia sat with her profile to him, perched in the armchair with her knees drawn to her chest, arms wrapped around her shins, rocking back and forth.

He walked into the kitchen, set down the bags and unloaded the items onto the counter.

"How are you feeling, dear?" he asked.

She gave no reply, only teetered slowly and stared at the TV.

The flat had an open floor plan, and with her back now to him, Marty noticed Lydia's shoulders looked too narrow. A knobby ridge of vertebrae rippled beneath the pale skin of her neck. Already slim, she was losing weight fast, and the sight of her skeletal frame sent a shiver through him.

"How was your day?" He expected no reply.

Following Dubois' suggestions Marty devised a rudimentary plan of action. First, he unscrewed a tin labeled "goofer dust," a deep gray powder that supposedly consisted of graveyard dirt, snakeskin, plus other herbs and spices. Marty wondered if he'd just dropped fifty dollars on crumbled charcoal. He took out a new paint brush, stepped into the bathroom and swathed a thick stripe of dust across the beige walls, the shower stall, the mirror, and completed the perimeter on the bathroom door.

Marty passed back through the den, where Lydia had stopped rocking. Her head now rolled slowly about her shoulders like she was working out a crick.

From the bags he grabbed four thick, red cylindrical candles, adorned with the Virgin Mary, lit them and placed one at each corner of the bathroom. He'd picked up a package of eye hooks at a hardware store, and manually twisted the threaded points into the plaster of the four walls near the bathroom ceiling. From each of the four hooks he hung a small straw-made cross, hand-twisted and bound with brown vines.

Back in the den Lydia stirred with an agitated growl, a low, guttural sound like an animal that sensed a threat.

For the next step Marty hammered three 16D framing nails halfway into the jamb just outside the bathroom door. Lydia angled her head at the clamor, chest heaving. Marty fashioned a loop of nylon rope, draped it over the nails and bent them against the wall with the hammer to clench the rope in place.

He then pulled a fillet knife from a kitchen drawer along with a rectangular sharpening stone. He ran the stone along the blade's edge with a scraping sound.

"Lydia, you're the most beautiful woman I know," Marty said. "I love you deeply, and everything I'm about to do is in your best interest. I want you to know that."

A hoarse rumble came from deep in her throat.

"You're going to have to trust me." He stepped into the bathroom, wrapped his fist around the blade and pulled the knife out by the handle. He spread his fingers, and a thin crimson line opened on his palm, stinging and leaking blood. He dragged his hand along the walls, wiping a red swath along the gray band of goofer dust.

Marty returned to the kitchen and rinsed his hand beneath the running water. Then he cut off the faucet. Lydia jerked upright, back stiff, when he did. Her growling stopped.

Marty took a pair a scissors from the bag. He walked into the den. She faced him as he approached, watching warily his every step.

Lydia's eyes, blazing red with gunshot pupils, burned holes straight through him. That's how it felt, that she was looking not at him, but past him, and into the vast unknown. Her face had thinned, and her lips pinched into a small, bitter scar.

In the floor before the recliner was a pile of red fur and broken bones. Marty choked back a surge of nausea on realizing he'd found the cat. Lydia must have torn the dead thing to pieces, snapped its bones and plucked it into bite-size chunks, then collected the bits and morsels in an absurdly neat mound on the floor.

He took a deep breath, stepped over to the wall and lifted the TV's power cord. He snipped it in half. The snowstorm on the screen went quiet.

Lydia gasped. Her nostrils flared and her hands began to shake. Her shoulders rose with huffing breaths. Marty braced himself for her to pounce.

Instead, Lydia slithered over the arm of the recliner. She slipped over its side and crawled on hands and knees across the floor toward the bathroom, her dingy robe flowing behind. The two running faucets in the sink and tub remained the only source of that dissonant hiss that seemed to compel and obsess her so intensely. Dubois claimed the compulsion was a common phenomenon associated with demonic possession.

As Lydia creeped over the threshold, Marty sprang into action. He shot into the kitchen and grabbed the filet knife off the counter. Lydia rose to her feet in front of the bathroom vanity. Marty approached from behind and seized her wrist. He caught his reflection in the mirror as he slid the knife across her palm. She yelped and winced as he pressed his wound over hers, blending their blood. He kissed her cheek. She shrieked, her free-hand flying hook-like at his face. Marty dodged the claw and pushed her backward.

Hopping out of the room, he slammed the bathroom door. He looped the nylon rope over the doorknob, doubled it round and round, and cinched it tight against the bent framing nails. Lydia was now trapped in a circle of sacrificial blood and magic powder, cornered by signs of Christ, just like Dubois suggested.

She grunted and muttered inside, shaking the knob, pulling the door which stretched the rope—but it held.

Screams erupted from the bathroom. Mad gibberish, tongue-tied, garbled nonsense spewed from the top of her lungs. The door bowed and banged against the frame.

"What the *hell* are youuu dooooiiing!!" she screamed from the din of snarls.

He rushed to the kitchen and lit a large black candle on the countertop. From the final bag he took out a sheet of parchment on which Dubois had penned Lydia's name in some sort of special ink. Marty collected his wife's wedding rings from his pocket, dropped them onto the yellow paper and folded it around them.

Cursing and raging, Lydia crashed into the bathroom door with explosive bursts. The floor vibrated with each bash.

"Martin? Marty! You useless shit! Open this door! I've got a *surprise* for you!" Her voice sounded strangled and stretched, alien and ghastly.

He ripped a leather-bound book from his back pocket. With a flip of the wrist it fell open to the page Dubois had marked with a business card.

Two loud booms pounded the wooden door, and Marty heard it crack.

"Oh, Marty," Lydia croaked. "I broke my poor hand. Please open the door so I don't break the other."

Marty focused on the words the voodoo man had underlined. The first few stanzas were written in a nonsensical amalgamation of French, Latin and some other unfamiliar script. He garbled through the pronunciation, stumbling over his tongue, unaware what the words really meant.

More crashes at the door, and Lydia shrieked. "I just broke the other one, *Marty!*"

When he finally got to the English portion of the spell, Marty belted it out like a patriotic Pledge of Allegiance.

Light this candle
Let it shine

Marty finished with the command: "I banish the negative energy from Lydia Leigh Fetzer!"

The bathroom clattered, clanged and rattled from the direction of its far wall. Lydia was trying to flee through the window. It had been bolted with iron security bars by the property owners.

"Oh, honey ... Dear lover," she muttered in a ravaged voice. Three more metallic clashes shook the apartment. "You're making me hurt myself. I need out of this room. I don't like it here!"

With a thunderous crash against the bathroom door, the wood gave way and a few splintered shards sprouted into the den on Marty's side. With another crash, the crack in the door opened further and a beam of light punched into the dimly lit room.

"My hands aw bwoken," she mumbled. "You make me use mah head and mah face."

"In the name of God, I banish the negative energy from Lydia Fetzer!" Marty shouted, willing the door to hold just a little longer. "No more harm may come to her! This is my will! So blessed it be!"

The door bent and burst with the onslaught, the veneer delaminating into jagged fronds. Lydia growled and snorted beast-like as she powered through, splitting the wood wider with each flailing attack.

Marty touched the parchment to the lit black candle. "This is my will!" Tears brimmed in his eyes. This had to work. It just had to, damn it! "Be gone, demon! I banish your negative energy from Lydia Leigh Fetzer!"

The folded paper bloomed into flame. Marty dropped it onto the countertop as the fire grew and consumed it, blackening the parchment and curling its edges. Lydia howled in an ear-piercing pitch. The scream stretched over many long, insufferable seconds, her ruined voice spiraling then waning into silence. The ramming charges subsided. A sudden empty peace fell over the rental flat.

Marty crept closer to the bathroom. He peered inside through the football-sized cavity Lydia had bashed through, but didn't see her. Only the steady hiss of running water broke the stillness.

And ... the soft, light sobs of his precious wife.

"Lydia?" he whispered through the hole. "Can you hear me?"

A thin whimper came from the foot of the door.

"Lydia? Are you okay? How do you feel?"

With a sniffle she said breathlessly, "I'm huht. Huht bad. What happen?"

Her voice had lost the grind of shattered glass. She sounded again like his lovely bride, only wounded, scared, and in need of his help.

Frantically, he went to work on the nylon rope, tugging at the knot. All the tension had pulled it noose-tight. He grabbed the kitchen knife to cut it free of the knob. With the rope loose, the door still met resistance.

"Scoot back, baby, so I can come in."

She did, and Marty opened the door to a murder scene. Splintered wood and shards of glass lay strewn about like debris from a bomb attack. Blood was everywhere—the walls, the shattered mirror, glistening on the bent steel bars of the broken window.

Lydia sat on her haunches, back against the tub. She cradled her face in her hands, crying. Her fingers stuck out in every direction, hands crunched and gnarled into mangled rags.

"I don't remembeh, Mahty. What happen da me?"

She dropped her hands and looked up with her one swollen eye. The other eyeball spilled out of its socket and dangled down her shredded face. She was split open from forehead to chin, lips dangling, tongue lolling, her teeth just chips and dust.

Marty felt the floor ripple with turbulence. Vertigo stretched the walls tall then bowed them outward. Lydia's butchered visage zoomed in and out as he threw his hands to his head and screamed. Stumbling backward, arms reeling, he expected the floor to open beneath his feet and swallow him to hell. This nightmare simply could not exist on earth.

"Mawty," she said with pure innocence, pleading with an outstretched arm and its savaged stump for her husband's loving touch.

But Marty ran.

He dashed out of the flat.

He tumbled into his car.

Tears streaming down his cheeks, he cranked the engine and sped down the street.

***

Dawn was breaking as Marty cruised along the winding back-roads of Louisiana. Only the hum of the engine met his ears. He'd called an ambulance for Lydia hours ago and had driven around aimlessly ever since. And now that he'd finally shed his last tear, he cursed the world and the heavens and the gods and the demons for wrecking his life.

For ruining his wife.

His luck had run out.

Lydia had been such a beauty, the poor thing. But beneath her skin Marty had seen all that wet, chewed meat and cracked bone, oozing and unsalvageable. And he simply could not bear it.

Her love had taught him a valuable lesson, though, one for which he would forever be grateful. Marty learned that he had true talent, an inner quality that deserved to be adored and appreciated. And his money probably helped. So, he reasoned there would be other Lydias. Other Charla's, with those slinky gowns clinging to their curves. And surely they, too, would see all he had to offer.

He pressed the accelerator and zoomed onto an interstate on-ramp, heading back home to the rising sun of Trapper Valley, Alabama. A brighter day lay ahead.

To hell with New Orleans.

The End

Silver Bullet Lies

The blood-splattered woman who stumbled out of the woods brought a hush over my brother Macon's six-year-old birthday party.

Uncle Caleb and I had been playing horseshoes in the back yard, while Macon, wearing a toy eyepatch, clashed plastic swords with Dad, commanding him to walk the plank.

Then, I saw Aunt Lois drop her beer bottle and stare behind me. I turned and froze at the sight of the stranger stepping onto our lawn. In that moment, you could hear nothing but the soft whimpers that escaped the lady's lips. Next came the gasps from the rest of us, as the woman, naked as a deli hen, stretched out her arms and screamed for help.

Hands clapped over mouths, and Mom ran over to cover Macon's eyes. Most of the family had gathered for cake beneath a big tent we'd raised in the backyard. Dad and Uncle Caleb inched toward the lady with their fingers splayed out and trembling, like they wanted to bring her into the fold but dared not touch her pale, bare flesh.

Aunt Lois finally snapped into action, shrugged off her shawl, and went to wrap it around the poor girl. That gesture seemed to refocus our group from shocked confusion to emergency response mode. None of us knew what horrors in the woods the girl might be fleeing, but she had wandered onto family land in need of help. And she'd come to the right place.

Our family, the Ketchums, were a tightknit clan, but our protective nature extended beyond blood kin to the very land around us. Our roots ran deep in the town of Shady Brake, so we placed high importance on thwarting threats of malice and evil.

We were all staring at an obvious victim, knowing this to be a clarion call to our family that wrongs must now be righted.

"Get the guns," Dad said, giving voice to what I'm sure we were all thinking: Whoever or whatever had bedeviled the young redhead, now shivering in a folding chair as Mom and Lois nursed her wounds, was likely still lurking in the woods. And if some kind of predator had been in hot pursuit of her, then it might not be far away.

Now was the time to act.

My cousin Devin jogged back from around the house, having already retrieved his shotgun. Seventeen years old with a spider tattoo on his neck, Devin always seemed fairly pissed off, and now I suppose he'd found a worthy target for his anger. He charged into the pines at the edge of the lawn.

This all unfolded quickly on one of those chilly October afternoons when the moon hung high and full long before the sun had fallen. I knew time was ticking fast, but I dashed inside for my thirty-eight and a Maglite, knowing how dark the forest could be deep inside the shadows.

Armed with live rounds and a shared sense of purpose, Dad, Caleb, Uncle Earl, and my fat cousin Terry joined me in a skirmish line along the back property.

"Boys," said Grandma, who'd risen from her place at the head of the picnic table. We stopped and turned, because whenever Grandma spoke, we all listened. "I have a dark feeling today. The winds are whispering. Something is in motion. Keep your hackles up."

We marched into the woods to commence the hunt, leaving behind a dozen hotdogs charring on the grill and the shellshocked woman, who seemed unable to speak about the nature of her trauma.

We charged ahead hunting a phantom, chasing a guess, as the shadows grew longer and blacker. The tangled branches overhead choked off the sunlight, and I clicked on my Maglite sooner than I expected. I knew these woods well, which is why I tried to avoid them.

I trudged deeper into the rough, losing sight of Dad and the others. The view ahead was muddled at best, but I kept my eyes peeled and ears attuned to any noise other than the crackle of straw and twig beneath my boots.

"I got something over here!" Devin hollered from up ahead. "Dad, you out here? Earl?"

"I hear you, Devin," I answered.

"Yo!" shouted Caleb, who was Devin's daddy. "Keep talking, son. I'll follow your voice."

"Over here!" he said. "I found… It's… I found a body."

"A what?" Caleb said off to my left.

"A body." Devin sounded like he was right in front of me, past a throng of black oaks.

I fought through a snare of ground-level vines and smelled the coppery stink of blood. When I reached Devin, I found him sitting on a moldy log with his head in his hands. On the ground, ten feet down a slope, lay a red-stained blanket, scattered beer cans, and a human corpse with its torso torn open and guts strewn out. Based on the muscle structure and striped boxers, the victim had been male, although a thick coat of blood concealed his face and identity.

"Good lord," I said and shut my eyes, trying to blink away the image and somehow un-see it.

"Sound off!" Caleb called from behind us.

"Over here!" I said back.

Caleb rounded a tree and saw the mess. "Holy shit!" He rubbed at his eyes like they were malfunctioning. The big gap in his beard was his mouth hanging open. "What the hell coulda done that?"

I shook my head. Devin didn't answer.

Caleb holstered his pistol and rubbed Devin's scalp. "You okay, son?"

Devin sniffled and nodded.

Sundown was an hour away, but you wouldn't know it this deep in the thicket below that dense forest shade. Roughly a hundred yards downhill from here, the woods ended at a lake, where you'd be sure to find a canoe or rowboat belonging to the ill-fated lovebirds drawn to the quiet seclusion for their afternoon tryst. This wasn't the first time a couple had been caught on our land. But this was the first time anyone had been killed.

"Guys, there's something out here!" Terry's voice sounded some thirty yards back, and very afraid.

"What's up, Terry?" Caleb yelled and drew his gun. Dad filed in right behind him with his rifle.

"Something is crawling around out here." Terry's voice came from the far side of a hill. "An animal, I guess. It's growling. And I can smell it."

My cousin Terry was a good fella, but a steady diet of fried chicken and donuts had ballooned him to the size of a pontoon boat. Being the slowest of our lot, he'd fallen behind, just as I'd worried.

"Keep talking, Terry!" Caleb was moving back in Terry's direction.

"I'm over here!"

I heard Uncle Earl holler to Terry in his unmistakable drawl: "I'm headed your way, Terry. Try to flush the thing out!" Earl stepped out of the brush sporting knee-ripped jeans, a red flannel shirt, and a double-barrel Remington at eye level, ready to fire.

"Whatever it is, it's getting closer!" Terry yelled.

"I'm coming in hot!" Earl said. "Keep sounding off, so I know your location!"

"It smells like a dog!" Terry said.

"If you shoot at anything, make sure it ain't me!" Earl told him.

I had my Maglite trained on Earl some twenty yards ahead of me. He had his beam aimed at the hillside. But I couldn't spot Terry.

"I see it!" Terry screamed. "Oh my god, I see it! I see it!"

A gunshot cracked through the forest. A chill crept over me.

"Terry, you good?" Earl shouted.

Caleb rushed past me toward the hill. "Sound off, Terry! Where ya at?"

"It's on the move!" Earl called to us. "Some kind of animal flanking to my left! Fast as hell and moving behind the trees! I've lost sight of it, but it's headed your way, Caleb!"

Caleb's direction… That meant the animal was headed for me too. Some sick impulse tempted me to glance back at the dead man, but I held fast and raised the .38 alongside my light.

"I don't see anything," Caleb called.

"Me either," said Dad, who'd flanked to my right, following Earl.

"Anyone got eyes on it?" Caleb asked.

I stopped walking and listened. I tried to detect the faintest grunt or whiff of animal musk.

"God almighty," Earl said in the distance. "I found Terry."

"What's wrong?" Dad said. "What happened to him?"

I had my beam fixed on Uncle Caleb. He was fighting ahead through thorn and bristle, when a gray flash pounced and ripped him from my view.

"Caleb!"

I heard cussing and animal growls. I swept my light back and forth over the brush, then saw Caleb hoisted into the air by two hairy appendages. Caleb's face went white, and he kicked his feet in mid-air. He wrenched against the beast's grip, but the thing towered over twice his size and shoved him down onto his knees. It clawed at Caleb's scalp, yanking his head backward, then it opened its long jaws and bared huge teeth. In a snap, the creature bit through Caleb's neck, and my favorite uncle's head rolled off his shoulders and into a trench.

My blood went ice cold, and I could not move a single muscle. The thing dropped Caleb's body and crouched over it on the ground, as if to feed on the carcass. Then, it hesitated. It sniffed the air and peered up at me with hungry, yellow eyes.

I realized I faced one of those pivotal moments in life that would impact my very existence, all determined by how I chose to act in that singular instant. I had the will to fire my gun, and I wanted desperately to flee, but due to some strange disconnection, my body failed to act. My muscles refused to follow the very clear demands from my brain. As the creature reared up on its haunches and lurched toward me, growling through moon-white fangs that drooled beneath a black, hairy snout, I stood motionless and utterly petrified with fear.

A blast of gunfire rattled me back to my senses. A second blast came with a muzzle-flash. I spun around to run away but tripped and fell flat onto the ground. I got a face full of leaves and expected those monster claws to rake right through the flesh of my back, but instead I heard the rack of a pump-action shotgun.

BOOM!

I saw my Maglite and snatched it from the dirt as Devin racked his gun again.

BOOM!—He blasted something on the ground just a few feet away.

Thank God for angry teenagers.

I pulled myself off the forest floor and tried to gather my thoughts—terrified, relieved, and grateful to my cousin.

"Son?" It was my dad, rushing up and catching his breath. "Son, you all right? Good Lord in heaven…" He threw an arm around my shoulders and squeezed, and this was special because he was not an expressive man. I hugged him back.

"I'm okay," I lied to spare him anything else to worry about. I was a wreck. "I'm okay."

He stepped back and leaned his head against a tree.

This had nearly been my very last day to share with the old man, the significance of which fell over me like a lead blanket.

Devin hadn't been as lucky. He ripped through the brush to get where his dad lay and let out a cry that must have carried for miles.

I felt sick.

"Look at this," Earl said as we walked up and stood over Devin's kill. "You seeing what I'm seeing?"

I pulled next to him and shone my light in the direction that Earl was staring. Dad stepped up too, and we all stood around gaping with our mouths open. Devin had blown the creature to bits, leaving little more than a meat pile where its head had been, but that's not what Earl had meant when he asked what we were seeing.

The body laying before us was changing. The fingers of the corpse twitched and shortened, and its long claws receded. The legs shivered and shuddered as the joints shifted and the bones morphed. The gray fur that covered the creature thinned and dissolved like cotton candy in water, as the thing on the ground transformed from a mangled beast to a bullet-ravaged man, still faceless, but familiar in form and absolutely unexplainable in nature.

"What the hell did I just see?" Dad asked in a tone I knew to be genuine disbelief.

The Ketchums were reasonable people but far from naïve about the mysteries of the universe and our smallness in the scheme of things—especially after everything we'd witnessed in Shady Brake over several generations. This area had a rich and peculiar history. But knowing that didn't make it any easier to swallow such strange new encounters when one would rear its head.

"It's just like in the movies," Earl said, as if to demonstrate how he and I were thinking on the same track.

When I'd seen the body start to change, my mind went reeling like an old VCR on rewind. Earl was only partly right, though, because what we'd witnessed was *not* just like the movies. According to the films I'd seen, werewolves could indeed shift from man to beast, but they could only be killed by a silver bullet. That latter notion had been disproven by the heavy-gauge lead shot that had splattered the thing's face—and the mess on the ground showed no signs of getting up to kill again.

Still, the recognition that Devin had killed a wolf-man carried grim implications with all sorts of horrifying possibilities. These thoughts must have gripped my dad, too, because he grabbed my shirt and tugged me back in the direction of the house.

"The others," he said. "We've got to get back there. Now!"

We all rushed back homeward with a renewed sense of urgency. We plowed through brush and branch and called out for our loved ones, as the sky darkened and thunder rippled. No storm had been forecast, though, and the change in weather gave me a sinking feeling.

Dealing with a werewolf brought crucial questions: Was more than one killer afoot? Could an entire pack of wolves be surrounding our house? Which of the "movie rules" were true and which were silver-bullet lies?

One idea I couldn't shake: According to popular lore, anyone who survived a werewolf attack would be cursed to change as well, transforming into one of those flesh-hungry creatures who hunt for prey by the light of the moon.

We'd left one of those victims in the care of our family.

These thoughts jangled through my brain as we raced home, my heart pounding in my chest. Dad's breathing came in short, sharp bursts, which worried me. I turned back to tell him to slow down. Stubborn old man wouldn't listen.

Finally, I made it out of the pines to our back yard. Red and blue balloons bounced in the wind from strings tied to our tent. Smoke snaked up from the coals on the grill. Nobody was in sight. Mom and Lois must have brought the woman inside the house.

A flash painted everything white. Thunder exploded right above us.

I dashed for the back door. It flung wide open as a gray shape shot outside, thumped onto the ground, and rolled across the lawn with a yelp. The thing growled and scrambled onto its paws. The creature spun back around, shook its head, and glared at the house. Then, it rose onto its hind legs, clawed at the air, and roared.

Not this time. Without wasting a second, I lined up my revolver at dead-center mass of the thing and touched the trigger.

"Wait!"

I stopped, because whenever Grandma spoke, we all listened.

My grandmother stepped through the doorway and onto the brick stoop with a hawk-like expression and eyes that blazed like the fires of hell. That's when I understood the storm around us. The clouds always gathered when Grandma was angry.

"She's mine," Grandma said, scowling at the creature.

I lowered my gun and took several steps backward. Dad, Devin and Earl rushed up and saw what was going on. They followed my lead. We all backed up.

The creature did not cower, though. It seemed to grow in girth and stature. It lifted its head and gave a baying howl at the angry sky. Then, it turned its yellow eyes back to Grandma. The beast had yet to learn its lesson.

The words she spoke to the thing could sting your ears and poke your brain. They were alien sounds recited with a weird, ethereal rhythm that invoked a timeless power of some ancient origin.

The clouds swirled, and the party balloons broke loose and flew away. A stiff wind churned through the yard, toppling chairs and ripping the tent canvas. Grandma's hair came untied and whipped about her head like a mane of silver flames. She parted her hands and raised them over her head.

The wolf creature growled and lunged for her.

Grandma brought her hands together in clap. A blinding explosion made the world go white.

***

Sometime later I found myself on my back, gazing at the stars of a clear night sky. Dad was brushing himself off, and Grandma was sitting on the stoop, leaning against the guardrail. All the action had taken a lot out of her.

My ears were still ringing. I stood up and brushed off charred bits of werewolf carcass from my clothes. The mess was everywhere. Grandma's lightning bolt had done a real number on the thing.

I knew right then—this would be one of those times when nobody outside the Ketchum family would ever believe a word of this.

"Is Mommy okay?"

When I heard Macon's tiny voice, a wave of relief washed over me. Thank God, my little brother had made it out alive. Macon crawled out from his hiding place beneath the picnic table.

That good feeling faded quickly, though, because he'd asked a damned good question. Where was Mom?

Macon limped over to where I stood alongside Dad, Devin and Earl. His pirate eyepatch was gone. His Superman T-shirt had been slashed, and claw marks bled from his shoulder. I gave him a hug and looked at my father.

I'll never forget the way Dad looked at Macon, looked at me, and then looked down at this rifle.

The End

In the Shadows of the Trees

Down a long and winding forest trail at the end of a lonely country road lived a solitary man of a primal nature. The hermit Everett Chesterfield smelled of piss from the pot beneath his bed and of whatever he'd last killed to eat. He wiped himself with leaves and picked his teeth with twigs. He cursed and spat at every man and leered at women from the forest at night. His small, scrap-built shack held a rusty, bent roof and leaned on crumbling block piers in the belly of an ancient marsh on the outskirts of Shady Brake, Alabama.

Most people paid him no attention. Most folks never encountered him. But Paul Ackerman and Ben Cowdy did. It all began one sweltering August afternoon when they got drunk and went mud-riding.

Having no money for a nice new UTV, they had fashioned the dune buggy in Paul's garage from the frame of an old Volkswagen Beetle that was peeled of its paneling and souped-up with off-road tires and high-impact suspension. The buggy bounced and rambled along a trickling creek bed while the two teens hooted and hollered, chugging cheap beer and treating every bump as a daredevil stunt ramp.

They did not see a harried Everett Chesterfield chasing down the love of his life.

They did not hear the girl screaming as she fled.

Weaving and winding deep inside the trench, flanked by tall earthen banks, the engine buzzed and the boys laughed as they made a sharp turn to follow the path.

It happened in a blink.

They rammed over a ragged shape that yelped and rolled beneath the wheels on the driver's side.

Paul slammed his foot on the brake, skidding to a stop with a spray of mud. He cut off the engine.

"What was that?"

Ben, the passenger, had spilled his Milwaukee's Best on the sudden stop. Dust settled on his damp, black Slayer t-shirt. He flicked beer off his hands. "I don't know. A scarecrow?"

"In a creek bed?"

They looked back, but a jutting bank obscured the view of the way they had come.

Paul, a tall, lean kid with a shaved head, hopped out of the buggy and rounded the corner. Ben jogged around to join him.

"Holy shit," Paul said.

In the orange dirt lay a young girl, motionless and unbreathing, with her head turned nearly backward. Her eyes, open but unaware, gazed at nothing, and a trickle of blood leaked from her nose. With such a skeletal frame and deathly complexion, she'd evidently been of ill health and thus an easy kill.

Ben, a thick boy with a square jaw and wavy black hair, tugged at the collar of his shirt. He staggered a few steps then grabbed a tree root to steady himself. His eyes watered. He leaned forward and vomited beer and foam. "She's dead," Ben stammered through a cough, beer dripping from his nostrils. "Oh my god, she's dead. We are so screwed!"

Paul teetered on his feet. He raised both hands to his head and looked up, staring through the groping tree branches and into the blue sky. He stood that way for a long moment, just gazing at the heavens. "Good Lord," he finally said.

"What do we do? What the hell do we do?"

"Christ, I don't know." Paul began pacing back and forth, wringing his hands. "I mean, she came out of *nowhere!* Why was she out here in the middle of the woods?!"

"Our lives are completely over," Ben put his fingers to his temples. "Our entire lives are over. They'll throw us in jail."

"It wasn't my fault!" Paul's voice cracked.

"Doesn't matter. We've been drinking all day. Nobody'll believe us." Ben made a growling noise that grew to a frustrated scream. "They'll probably charge us with murder!"

"Manslaughter."

"Jail, either way."

"I can't go to jail." Paul knelt over the girl. A tear dripped from his nose. "I just can't."

"We go report this right now while we're smelling like a brewery, we're going *straight* to prison. Bet on it," Ben said.

Paul swept dirt away from the girl's arms. "What the hell?" He wiped his nose and looked at Ben. "Hey, look at this."

Ben walked to the body and leaned over. The girl wore a long, ragged dress tailored from decades past, the fabric thin and faded with pale yellow tulips in a repeating pattern. Bruises and scrapes covered her exposed skin. Her wrists were bound with twine, and abrasions circling her ankles suggested they had been tied, too.

"Jesus Christ," Ben said.

"Who would've done that?"

Ben shook his head. "Where do you think she was running to?"

"Home, probably," Paul said. "What do you think she was running *from?*"

The two boys shared an uneasy grimace. Both stood up and backed away from the girl. They looked around their surroundings, wary of watchful eyes. The green forest, thick with brush and vine, loomed over the thirsty creek and netted them in shadow. A wandering squirrel shook the leaves overhead. Toads croaked nearby.

"We gotta make a decision," Ben said. "Take her to the cops or leave her."

"You recognize her?"

"No."

"I think it's Lilly Friese," Paul said.

"Who's that?"

"Lilly Friese ... Remember all those flyers around town? The girl who went missing a couple months back?"

Ben stared at the body. "Oh, shit... I think you're right."

Paul wiped snot running from his nose. "I think I just ran her over."

All the locals had been gripped by the story: A local honor student had taken an afternoon jog along a quiet suburban street and vanished without a trace. Still fresh with mystery, Lillie Friese's disappearance remained the talk of the town to the very day.

"Maybe we should hide her," Ben said.

Paul eventually agreed.

***

From a thick patch of brush overlooking the hillside some sixty feet away, Everett Chesterfield watched the drama unfold. He dug his nails into the flesh of his thigh and bit his tongue so hard it bled. He'd really loved that one, such a pretty thing.

He studied the boys' faces and their machine. It was the type of machine they would tow back home on a trailer. He knew where all the kids parked their trucks near the mouth of the trails. That's where he'd find their vehicle, and that's how he planned to track these two boys down, one at a time.

***

In the hours to follow, shame clung to Paul Ackerman like skunk musk. He was sure that everyone else could smell the guilt all over him. He noticed the shifty eyes of the people he passed, from Mrs. Nettie who rang him up at the gas station to the pimple-faced kid who handed him his fries at the Burger Hut. Paul had killed a girl and buried her beneath rotting limbs and leaves under a fallen tree trunk. And somehow everybody knew what he'd done. Through some strange telepathy, everyone in town had learned what happened and had him pegged as the culprit—he was sure of it.

"Hi, honey," Paul's mother greeted as she came through the kitchen door with a sack of groceries.

He sat at the kitchen table staring blankly at a plate of cold French fries. He'd lost his appetite.

"How'd you spend your Saturday?" she asked.

Maybe she hadn't yet learned of the crime the same way everyone else had. Poor Mom: destined for disappointment. Just like Dad, God rest his soul.

"Nothing much. Muddin' with Ben."

She placed the groceries on the countertop, gave him a smile, and went about stocking the cabinets. "You boys have fun?"

That shattering moment of impact played on a loop in his mind—the ragged shape flashing across his vision, then a quick, startled human shout. In that instant he'd stolen away a young girl's life, and he couldn't seem to shake away the moment. She'd come out of nowhere, and when he'd knocked her from the present, he'd stamped out all her dreams for the future, and those stolen moments tore at him. Adding insult to injury, he'd then concealed the body and effectively erased Lilly Friese from all existence — the ultimate act of destruction and cowardice.

Now, he hated himself for all of it.

"It was okay, I guess," he told his mother.

He looked down at his food but all he saw was a dead girl, who lay bound and broken.

***

Paul and Ben had met at the trailhead on the day of the accident. Paul drove a 90s model F-150 pickup, rigged with a trailer to tow the buggy. Ben drove a dented turquoise Corvette. And Everett Chesterfield knew the cars of the Shady Brake townsfolk as well as he knew all the best fishing holes and deer fields. The cars carried the girls, and he knew the girls from the windows of their homes.

The Corvette sometimes carried a young fat girl. The truck sometimes carried a pretty older woman.

Everett knew where to find the boys' two vehicles. He knew exactly which houses they matched.

***

Ben's mom worked evenings at a local diner. His father worked as an electrician, currently down south wiring a commercial building. Nights at the Cowdy house were quiet these days. Sometimes Paul would stop by with a sixer, and other times Ben would go cruising with Shelly Higgins, a large girl with big breasts who liked to get naked. But Ben usually stayed alone. He'd picked up a few neighborhood lawns to mow to make a little cash, but usually just watched TV, played video games or drove over to Lake Matheson to fish for crappie off the bank. For the most part, it had been a quiet summer, his final three-month vacation before senior year at Trapper Valley High.

Life had been slow lately but easy, and the terrible thing that happened yesterday had been a particularly nasty hiccup. Still, it was a distraction that Ben hoped to quickly put behind him, never speak of again, and eventually convince himself had never happened.

On returning to his house with a sack full of burgers, however, that particular hope shattered with a thunderclap. Ben froze when he saw what hung from the front door of his house.

A long, rusty knife stuck out from the white-painted wood.

He dropped his cheeseburgers.

Pinned against the door by the pitted blade was a swath of thin cloth with a familiar pattern of faded yellow tulips—the same threadbare fabric that had wrapped Lilly Friese.

Ben felt as though writhing roots the size of pythons had suddenly erupted from the earth to wrap his legs and pull him beneath the ground, leaving him no hope of ever escaping.

***

Paul stared at the slit in the white-painted wood as he knocked on the Cowdys' front door. Ben opened the door with a beer in hand. A few dribbles spotted his pale blue t-shirt, emblazoned with the slogan: *Eat More Smoked Meats*. He thumbed at the slit in the wood and nodded, then ushered Paul inside the house without a word.

Paul took a seat on the couch and immediately dropped his head into his hands. "I knew we'd get found out," he said in a deadpan. "Go ahead. Give me the details."

Ben stood in the center of the living room and swayed slightly as he finished his can of Coors. He walked over to a TV tray on the coffee table, picked it up and brought it to Paul.

"Here's the knife," Ben said. He placed the tray in Paul's lap.

After a moment, Paul gingerly lifted the wood-handled hunting knife, grimy and corroded as if found in a junk pile, and examined the soft patch of cloth speared over the blade.

"Somebody found her body," Paul muttered.

"That's a safe bet."

Ben stepped over to the bay window of the dimly lit room. He parted the blinds to peek outside the rear of the house, which backed against the woods.

Paul closed his eyes and gave a deep, weary sigh. "I'm going to jail. I'm going to prison. That's my future."

Ben walked to the refrigerator, pulled out two more beers and returned with one for his friend. "We're both going down."

"Naw. I'll take the heat." Paul grabbed the Coors. "It was my fault what happened. I was driving. No sense in both of us going down."

"I helped hide the body," Ben said.

Paul wiped his nose. "Yeah, but nobody knows that but—" He stopped his thought.

"Nobody but you and whoever jammed a knife in my door. I appreciate the gesture, buddy, but me and you are both on the hook for this one."

Ben pulled the rope on the blinds, which sandwiched up to reveal a gridded bay window overlooking a small patio. He stared outside with narrowed eyes and a grim expression as though searching for some threat beyond the line of his property.

Paul joined him at the window. Dusk was settling over Shady Brake, and the shadows stretched long. The Cowdys' well-maintained lawn thickened with thatch and weeds along its outer edge, then the wilderness took hold, climbing a craggy hill of tall black trees skirted by a sea of kudzu. That insatiable vine overtook the hillside like a suffocating plague and covered the forest floor in a mysterious web of leathery scales. The vast blanket of green leaves draped old stumps and fallen branches, creating alien shapes as though huge Jurassic beasts were emerging from the foliage for an ambush—a monstrous scene from the midnight sci-films Paul used to watch with his father before the Big C took him away.

"Got any guesses who might know our secret?" Ben said.

"Not any good ones." Paul didn't want to state his suspicion. His only idea seemed a little far-fetched, a little too "midnight movie"—but from a horror film rather than science fiction. "You?"

After another moment of studying the woods, Ben looked at him and nodded. "Just one. And it makes all the sense in the world."

"Okay. Who?"

"You know who. That crazy bastard who lives in the hills. Ol' what's-his-name ... the guy who rummages through garbage cans and steals old ladies' cats."

As it turned out, Ben shared Paul's suspicion. He was right that it only made sense. They'd been worried about a hunter with a dog sniffing out the body, but for someone to tie them to the killing so quickly meant they'd been caught in the act. Someone hiding in the woods must have seen them commit the crime.

Only one man in town was known to lurk in the woods. Everyone steered clear of a hermit named Everett Chesterfield, wary of catching a disease and afraid of the rumors about what he did at night. He survived by hunting, foraging and theft; such was the assumption of the rare few who ever paid him a passing thought—namely the local police and wary property owners. Viewed as a public nuisance and an embarrassment to the close-knit community, he remained for decades shunned and maligned, the villain of spooky campfire tales that local kids told to scare their friends.

And then came yesterday's incident deep in the pines, where nobody wandered without motorized transportation—except for that one weird man who everyone hated.

"Chesterfield," Paul said. "Everett Chesterfield."

Ben nodded again. "That's him—the watcher ... The watcher in the woods."

"You think he saw us?"

Ben rolled his tongue around the inside of his cheek, then said, "That's all I can figure."

"But Lilly Friese ..."

Ben looked at him, and Paul read his mind. Everett Chesterfield had snatched the poor girl and kept her tied up like a sex doll—or something like that. She'd managed to escape, and they'd run her down mid-flight in the mud buggy. Chesterfield must have been in pursuit when it happened.

"I think we killed his girlfriend," Ben said.

"His prisoner."

"Same thing, to a crazy person."

The implications of it all darkened Paul's mind like a gathering storm. "Everett Chesterfield wants revenge."

Ben stepped back from the window. He chewed on his lip, crushed the empty beer can and tossed it onto the TV tray with the knife. "I'm guessing that's the message he intended to send. I don't think somebody like that goes to the police to get their justice ... Somebody who kidnapped a girl. Someone with something to hide."

Paul closed his hands into fists. "Someone like *us*."

Ben went to the fridge for more beer. The guy didn't usually drink so much, not unless he was fishing or mud-riding, but Paul figured it was a means of escape and couldn't fault him for it.

"Thass right," Ben said. "Someone like us."

"So what should we do?" It was a question without a good answer, and Paul felt dumb for asking it.

"I'm gonna load my dad's gun and keep my eyes open," Ben said with a mild slur. Booze brought out the drawl in his southern accent. "And I figure you oughtta do the same."

The suggestion sounded reasonable, but Paul's dad hadn't left him a gun. The thought of his mother home alone sent a shiver through him. Unguarded and unaware of a mounting threat, she could be a sitting duck. After all, if Everett Chesterfield could figure out where Ben hung his hat, what's to stop him from tracking down the address of his partner in crime?

"I've got to go," he told Ben. "Mom will be home soon. I want to check on her. You let me know if you see any sign of him. I'll call you in a couple of hours."

Ben nodded slowly with a boozy smile. "Ten-four, buddy," he said, with eyes pink and watery. "I'll keep a lookout."

***

Ben watched Paul drive away. He shut the front door.

With no more company and no one else at home, the house seemed particularly quiet, even hostile. And the damn thing had windows everywhere. Ben had never paid attention to how the average home was Swiss-cheesed with windows until this very moment, and the layout of his family's modest single-level abode felt particularly vulnerable at the moment. He felt like a bird in a cage watched by anyone and everyone, watched by someone who could reach inside and crush the bird if they wanted to be cruel.

Ben stumbled through his home, drawing curtains and closing blinds, blocking out the prying eyes of the watcher in the woods. He gritted his teeth as he did so, because enmeshed in his creeping dread was a simmering booze-addled anger. Maybe he'd buried a body but he hadn't been at the wheel when the girl was killed. The whole mess with Lilly Friese wasn't his fault, and he didn't plan on paying a price for a crime he didn't actually commit—not to the authorities or to some crazy ol' coot in the forest. And if that nutty bastard shows his ugly face around here again…

Ben closed the last blind and remembered the gun.

His dad stored the forty-four in a locked tool cabinet inside the detached garage next to the house. The outbuilding served as his pop's private retreat, where he'd suck down beer, listen to talk-radio, and obsessively polish the body of an engine-less '69 Mustang that he kept in an endless state of rehabilitation.

Ben grabbed a key from a kitchen drawer and walked out to the garage. As he pushed it into the lock, he found the door ajar. It opened freely with a slight squeak. His dad was bad about keeping the thing locked, but then there was no worry of someone driving off with his prized possession. Still, Ben had told him that while home break-ins were a rarity in Shady Brake, outbuildings were a different story as teens roamed the neighborhoods late at night in search of liquor to steal—or maybe a gun. Ben knew this because he'd done it himself on many occasions. Just last month, he snatched a fifth of Jim Beam from the Blackwell's storage shed two streets away.

Darkness painted the garage. When Ben hit the wall switch, a single naked bulb buzzed weakly at the end of a rafter-mounted cord. The dim light cast an orange glow across the shining car body, but deep pools of black shadow ate the corners of the room and blighted the many shelves cluttered with tools and junk.

Ben threw his hand to his nose. The place reeked like urine and rot. The stench hung so thick in the hot air it was almost overpowering. What the hell had Dad been doing in here? Ben suspected a plate of spoiled food hid somewhere in the mess, probably crawling with maggots.

Just get in and get out.

A rolling metal closet in the corner of the small building held the forty-four. The key to the lock dangled ridiculously from the corner of the closet door, and Ben often told his dad that he might as well add a big bow and a plate of cookies for the eventual thief.

He lifted the key-ring from its hook and fidgeted its round nose into the circular keyhole. His dad's gun packed a hell of a punch, and if old Everett Chesterfield—

A starburst of pain punched through his lower back.

His face slammed the metal cabinet and bounced off. Piercing force shoved further into his right kidney. His cheek again met cold metal with a clang. Ben slapped his palms against the double doors and shoved away from the closet. He spun around but screamed with shearing agony, because whatever had hit his back remained *inside* his back.

His twisting motion wrenched the long stick away from whatever figure stood behind him. The wood handle banged across the red Mustang hood, and Ben realized he'd been stabbed.

In the sparse light he saw a face, a twisted goblin face with jagged black teeth and a bloodthirsty scowl that launched at him with two twisted talons. Ben raised fists to shield himself, and Everett Chesterfield grappled with his forearms, hissing and sneering. Smaller than Ben but wiry, he leveraged a leg against the Mustang's bumper and pushed Ben again into the locked closet.

Ben's torso twisted against hard metal. The prongs of the weapon angled deeper into the flesh of his back. He howled as his insides tore with hot, sticking pressure. He hit his knees. His head rammed the door with a blinding thud, and he went to the floor face-down.

Ben clenched his jaws in a spike of fury, and in that instant wanted nothing more than his dad's gun shoved deep inside this filthy bastard's mouth. He pushed himself up and—

"*Aaaack!*"

He felt the spear rip out of his back. A bright explosion of pain came with a new blow between the shoulder blades. A cluster of cuts plunged into him like the spear had many blades. His chin smacked the concrete floor.

More blows rained down. Ben's body convulsed.

The last one ripped through his neck with a pinched gagging sensation like he'd swallowed a fork. A wave of panic hit him as he gasped for breath but choked, the air gurgling in his throat. Pressure built in his brain. Blood pounded through his eardrums. Then it slowed, the rapid flow waning to a trickle.

Everett Chesterfield pulled the dripping weapon out of Ben's flesh. He dropped it into the dark pool spreading on the floor in front of his face.

Ben struggled to keep his eyes open as he heard his killer rummage through the garage, shoving stuff onto the floor, and slamming open the closet doors. The thief he'd warned his dad about had finally arrived.

He stared at the tool that had brought him down and recognized its shape. Dad had taught him how to make one back in his Boy Scout days. Its long handle had been cut from a hardwood tree branch with the last six inches quartered lengthwise, whittled at the tips, and spread apart by dowels and twine into four sharpened prongs.

As Ben's eyes fell closed, his heart sank at the knowledge that he'd been speared to death with a homemade frog gig.

***

"You can't fool me, Mister," Paul's mom said from the doorway of his bedroom. The yellow light of the hallway framed her nightgown silhouette. "I can tell something's bothering you. What's on your mind?"

Paul sat up in bed and took a swig from the glass of water on the nightstand. His mother was right, of course. Since his father's passing, the two of them had grown closer than ever, and Paul sometimes got the feeling his mom could actually read his mind. She had the shrewdest of motherly intuition, which made it pointless to deny what she knew.

"It's nothing," he lied. "Just thinking about Dad, I guess. I miss him."

"Oh, honey." She walked into the room and sat beside him, hooking her arm around his waist. She leaned over and kissed his forehead. "I know. I miss him every day. But always remember what I've told you. That he's here with us. He's always with you and me both, as long as we keep him in our hearts."

This was a conversation they'd had many times, and he felt cheap for invoking his dad's death just to deflect her suspicion.

When she retired to her room, Paul stretched out on the mattress and stared at the dark bedroom ceiling, his mind clouded with grim thoughts and pestering questions. Did his father see from heaven what he'd done to Lilly Friese? What did his dad think of him now?

What did God think of him? God was always watching.

Just like the eyes in the shadows could watch him — the shadows just outside his home, which backed against a thick throng of maples and pines that walled a deep hollow in the forest.

Was his home being watched at this very moment? Was Everett Chesterfield actually out for revenge? How far would the crazy bastard go to get even, and who all would he target?

Paul wanted to go sleep next to his mother. Part of him wanted to be held like a baby. Another part meant to guard her. But she would consider that odd and unusual behavior, would want to know why he was being so protective, and Paul simply didn't have an explanation he was willing to give.

So, he stayed in bed, deathly still, listening in the blackness for the faintest sound or any suspicious noise that might indicate the presence of an intruder. He listened quietly for hours.

Until he fell asleep.

***

Paul awoke with the thin light of dawn tinting the room a hazy blue. He hadn't intended to sleep. He sat bolt upright and looked at the nightstand alarm clock.

7:10 AM.

On a typical Monday morning he'd hear the tinny voices of chuckling morning-show hosts humming from his mom's little kitchen countertop TV. He'd hear her padding around the house, preparing for the workday and feeding the cat. Faucets would turn on and off, and eventually the hair dryer would blare. Sometimes she'd call her sister on speakerphone to chat while she got ready.

This morning he heard nothing. An unsettling silence hung in the air around him.

Paul leapt from the covers and bounded downstairs. Quiet stillness pervaded the home, and he saw no sign of his mother's typical morning activities.

"Mom!" he called. "Mom? You here?"

The lack of reply quickened his pulse.

"Mom?!" Paul shouted as he shot back upstairs and down the hall. He threw open the door to his mother's bedroom and swooned at the sight.

A spear of some sort—a homemade weapon like a frog gig—stood upright in the center of the bed. It pinned a red-splotched cloth to the mattress. With hands trembling, Paul took two cautious steps closer to examine it. He recognized the swath of blue fabric and the familiar slogan visible through dark, red stains: *Eat More Smoked Meats*

His heart dropped into his stomach.

In a rush he stumbled from the room and into his own, where he climbed into a dirty pair of jeans. He shoved his feet in his shoes and rushed downstairs.

He got the buggy loaded in record time. With a clang of the trailer gate, he went tearing down the road in his pickup. Ben hadn't answered his phone. As Paul rounded the corner to his friend's street, he saw flashing ambulance lights. A platoon of police cars surrounded the Cowdys' place. Anguish gripped him and twisted, and he nearly swerved into a ditch. He clenched his teeth and managed to steady the weaving trailer, cruising by the scene in a cold sweat.

Paul's vision clouded with tears, and the world around him grew chilly and foul. He somehow knew that he would never speak to Ben again. Ben was gone. He knew that to be a cold, irrefutable truth, as reliable as death and decay.

And Paul's mother was now in the grips of the same devil that had taken his friend. He had only one fleeting hope, and that was to find the damned thing at its fabled shack deep down in the thickest woods of Shady Brake.

That's how he had to think of Everett Chesterfield; not as a person but as a *thing*, as a vile, sadistic animal that posed a threat to all that was good and decent. He had to think of the hermit as a thing and not a human because he planned to kill it. He planned to rid the world of the walking cancer.

His mission was clear: Find his mother, rescue her and slay the beast. He could consider no other option.

His mission's execution, however, depended on hearsay and dumb luck. Hopefully the old shack was located right where the stories suggested. With any luck, that's where he'd find his mom, scared but untouched. That particular scenario struck him as awfully sunny and neat, but Paul gripped the wheel and soldiered onward, speeding down the bumpy road to the outskirts of Shady Brake. To turn back was unthinkable. After all, this was a mess of his making.

"You'll be the man of the house," his dad had told him from his bed in the hospital. *"I'm counting on you."*

Paul had let his father down and knew he had only one shot at redemption. He pegged the buggy's gas pedal and tightened his fist around his weapon of convenience, the inch-thick tire iron that lay across his knees.

He came to the end of the road, where the asphalt petered away to a worn, barren path beneath a shadowy tunnel of brush and brambles. He dropped the buggy off the trailer, threw the tire iron into its passenger seat, hopped inside, and blazed down the trail with the wind in his face and branches whipping his bare arms. He bounded the buggy over rocks and trenches, rattling his teeth and realizing the element of surprise was not on his side.

His breath caught in his throat as the branches eventually cleared for sight of a leaning gray building perched on blocks in a small clearing. Surrounded by bizarre bone sculptures and animal skulls perched atop leaning wood pikes, the place looked like the lair of a fairytale troll. As he pulled nearer, the spinning tires of the buggy slung mud in thick, brown fans. He motored around the little shack, fishtailing, and spying for signs of life or danger. From outside he could detect none, but he did spy Ben's dented Corvette half sunk in the mud at the edge of the woods.

Paul spun the machine in a donut and idled in front of the plywood door. He grabbed the tire iron and climbed outside, leaving the engine running.

All his guts seemed to shrivel and liquefy somewhere down near his testicles. He scanned his perimeter, searching the thick wall of trees and snaking vines that engulfed the area. A hundred evil eyes could be watching him unseen, waiting for the perfect moment to spring a trap. But he hardened his war-face. He peeled back his lips in a stony grimace and forced a near-psychotic conviction to duty to the front of his mind. There were fates worse than death, like suffering a lifetime of shame.

Paul waded through the mud then climbed the cinderblock steps. He took a deep breath and kicked open the door.

The smell of death hit him in a wave. He arched backward from the odor. Flies buzzed out the doorway, and inside the darkened box he saw a crumpled figure bent in half. He nearly collapsed, then he recognized the dress. Faded tulips.

A gutted animal carcass, maybe a coyote, rotted on the floor next to two plastic buckets, one half full of water and the other with shit. The stench made him retch.

Movement to his right, and he raised the tire-iron. A filthy mattress lay on the floor. A nude woman lay curled on the mattress, bound by twine with a sack over her head. Her body trembled and glistened with sweat and filth, and she gave a whimper.

"MOM!" He dropped his weapon and worked the bag off her head. His mother's wild, wet eyes and quivering lip broke his heart, just as it sent a black fire of hate coursing through his veins.

"I'm here, Mom. I'm here." His voice broke despite his best efforts.

"Paul?" she croaked. *"Paul?!"*

He cut the twine with his pocketknife. He gathered his mother and wrapped a filthy blanket around her. Paul grabbed his tire iron, and they staggered out the door.

The rumble of the idling engine stopped as they stepped outside.

The sudden silence hit Paul like a bullet. He and his mother froze.

A rag-wearing vagrant with a patchy, whiskered face stood next to the buggy with his hand splayed open to show the key ring on his palm. He stared at Paul through cold gray eyes, twisting his hollow, filth-streaked cheeks and rotted mouth into a sneer.

Paul's mother gave a high-pitched whine and began to blubber at his side. She cowered against him. He'd never seen her act so infantile. He wrapped an arm around her and led her away from the buggy to the trail.

Paul fixed on the beady eyes of the scowling bastard Everett Chesterfield. He brandished the tire iron at him with a single hand but uttered not a word. His was a silent warning, and crystal clear: Fuck with us as we leave, and I'll bash your skull apart.

The muddy earth around the shack swallowed his shoes like a tar pit. His mother's bare feet disappeared in the muck with each step. They slogged with grueling effort as the hermit only stood and watched. And Paul didn't like the way he just stood and watched.

As the mud shallowed and stiffened, and they gained a better foothold, their pace quickened. They neared the path, and Paul had a glimmer of hope.

The crack of a gunshot snuffed that glimmer.

"Run!" he shouted. "Run, Mom, run!" They lunged through the last of the mire.

Another gunshot fired from behind. Paul threw a glance over his shoulder to see Chesterfield trudging for them with a pistol in hand.

"Come on, Honey!" His mom yelled. She reached firm ground and padded up the trail with new vigor.

Another *POW!* and bark exploded off a tree to her right.

"Run, Mom!" Paul screamed. "Keep running!"

And she did.

Paul did, too, but his muddied boots weighed him down. With another gunshot crack, a sharp heat stabbed his thigh. He fell. The tire iron rolled out of reach.

He reached for his wound and drew back blood on his fingers. Blood spread over his jeans, hot and wet.

"*Paaauull!*" screamed his mother.

He shot a forceful look up the hill at her and roared, "Keep running! *Go!* Get help!"

Footsteps thumping closer told him that Everett Chesterfield had cleared the mire. As the stomp of Chesterfield's ratty boots drew up behind him, Paul gasped for breath and reached down to his sneakers, scooping up a palm full of caked mud from the toe.

The shadow of the hermit fell over him. Paul reared back with his right arm and slung the clump upward.

Brown splatter slapped the hermit in the eyes. He hissed and staggered backward. Paul pushed up and grabbed the man's crotch and twisted. Chesterfield howled and brought the gun down like a hammer. It glanced Paul's head.

With testicles in one hand, Paul drove his other fist into the bastard's breadbasket. Chesterfield folded over and fell with a spray of air through his black gums.

Paul's vision blurred at the corners. He swooned with a faint spell but bit his lip and focused. He grinded through the searing fire in his thigh and threw his body on top of the gasping man on the ground. Paul mustered a surge of strength and clutched the man's skull with both hands. He gave a roar that sent the birds above soaring as he plunged his thumbs with full force into the eye sockets of Everett Chesterfield's face. The old man's wicked scream filled the forest as Paul pushed deeper inward, harder and angrier. He wanted to touch brain in that shuddering head. Two soft-boiled eggs popped into his palms, and the warm soup that bubbled out of the two sockets felt like striking black gold.

Drained and weakened but still grasping two handfuls of something wet, Paul toppled off the moaning man beneath him. His muscles surrendered. He could barely move. He angled his head up the trail, but at first did not see his mother.

She had escaped.

He had saved her.

Yet, now she was coming back.

As the woods became gauzy, Paul cast a final look at Everett Chesterfield, who crawled blindly along the forest floor on his hands and knees, coughing and mewling. The old man pawed at his wounds and howled every time he touched the gooey red strands swinging down from his face.

The world dimmed. Paul's breath grew shallow, but he embraced a sense of peace and fulfillment because his mother, God bless her, was now safe. His father would have been proud.

And because that sonofabitch Everett Chesterfield would never again watch another Lilly Friese, or anyone else, from the shadows in the woods.

The End

Beware the Whammy

None of us believed in the old lady's curse until midnight. Until then, we thought she'd been off her rocker, just a crazy old bird pissed about her dead dog and shouting a lot of angry nonsense.

The three of us had been inspecting a few rundown properties in the marshy outskirts of a little backwater burg called Shady Brake. I'd visited many tiny Alabama towns much like it, the kind of place where nothing much happened but backroad drag races and Friday night cockfights. We worked for a real-estate development firm out of Birmingham, but all that remained of this forgotten neighborhood was a collection of small, crumbling homes with only a handful of occupants among them, each strapped by poverty or stricken by worse. The boss must've gotten some wrong intel, because many of these homes had clearly been built in a flood plain, and over the years the structures had buckled, bowed and molded.

We were cruising along in the company van when the mutt shot out from a snarl of bushes. It dashed right in front of us in a golden flash. I heard a bark and a thump, and Murphy hit the brakes. The van bucked as it rambled over the dog.

"What was that?" asked Hettinger, our co-worker, from the back seat.

My stomach turned over.

Murphy's face went pale. What happened wasn't his

fault, although the howling woman in rags who burst out of a nearby door seemed to think so. We pulled to the shoulder, and she rushed from a shotgun house with hands flailing and her long, white hair trailing all wispy like spider silk. We climbed out of the car as she knelt over the animal, an adult retriever mix that shivered on the ground, not quite dead.

The old lady quivered and moaned. "Oh, poor Sandy!" she said. "My poor precious Sandy! What have they done to you?"

Tears dripped from her chin, and the sight of it all tugged at me.

Another man, unshaven and dressed like a beggar, ran over, kneeled and put an arm around her. I wanted to step forward, to offer them aid, but I just stood there and watched, at a loss for how to help.

What happened next was over before I realized it. Hettinger pulled out a pistol and shot the dog.

BAM!

The sound stung me like a hornet. But an empty silence followed that went deep as a dry well.

He had shot the poor thing point-blank in the head. The dog went still. Murphy and I turned to each other, and I probably looked as dumbstruck as he did.

The old lady shuddered beneath the man's arm. The way she trembled in place, her entire body shaking, I half expected some sort of volcanic explosion to erupt right out of her shawl. The man raised his head first, and then she finally cast a glare up in our direction. The ice in her eyes gave me goosebumps.

"How could you?" she growled. "How could you do that?" She had a thick Southern drawl with a touch of foreign accent that I couldn't quite pinpoint.

The three of us each took a step back. I'd hoped the target of that withering gaze would stick with the other two:

Hettinger, the trigger-man, and Murphy, the driver. But she let me have it too, with those huge black pupils like two chunks of stove coal. As far as she was concerned, I was guilty by association.

"I'm so sorry, ma'am," Murphy said, his face slack. "The poor thing ... I tried to stop. I swear I didn't see it in time."

"And, you..." she hissed at Hettinger. He was the tallest of us, a new trainee with closely cropped red hair, a heavy brow and a severity beyond his thirty years.

"I had to do it, ma'am," he said. "The animal was suffering. It's a real shame, and I'm sorry. But I had to do what's right."

At that moment I noticed the sky darkening, clouds gathering overhead with the threat of rain. The day grew eerie and grim.

The old lady's scowl only hardened. I sensed a storm stir inside her just like it gathered above, and she shot us each that vengeful glare and said a strange word: "Whammy."

We looked at one another.

She said it three times, once to each of us, while staring us dead in the eye: *Whammy.*

Something about the sound of that word unsettled me deeply.

"Elnora!" gasped the man beside her. "What are you doing?!"

Elnora pushed up and rose to her feet. She stepped toward us, grumbled something, then lunged forward. She clutched Hettinger's hand. He tore it away. She grabbed my hand and Murphy's, but we retreated too. She raised her palms, gleaming red with the dog's blood. We each now had the blood on our skin.

Slowly she spun in a circle, tilting her head to the sky and whispering. The local man took a few steps back.

The woman spoke softly at first, reciting some

unfamiliar chant I couldn't quite make out. Then, as her voice rose:

"May a sparrow smash your window,
May your crops know blight and drought
May the midnight clock start ticking
May a whammy seek you out!"

Thunder rumbled in the distance as she repeated the rhyme, her voice rising to a screech.

"Three nights!" she cried, shaking her fists. "Three bites!"

Rain began to pour from the clouds. The wind tousled her hair like a nest of writhing serpents.

We rushed back to the van as the lady spat at us and told us to burn in hell. Her shouting devolved into crazed ranting—words I'd never heard spoken. As we piled in, she pounded on the side of the vehicle, bashing her fists into the paneling.

"What in blue blazes?" Murphy said

"Just drive," Hettinger yelled. "Drive!"

Murphy hit the gas.

It wasn't until we were back at the motel a couple exits up the Interstate that we found the markings on the side of the van. The woman had drawn some strange, circular symbol, smeared in blood and streaked by rain.

We needed to settle our nerves, and decided our best move was to pound some brews at the bar across the street.

***

We sat around a table in a dimly lit honky-tonk dive that served beer, burgers and hot wings. The place smelled like cigarettes and had brick walls decorated with automobile license tags. Willie Nelson sang "Whiskey River" through the stereo. Hettinger and I were plowing through our sandwiches, but Murphy just stared at his plate and poked at his chicken. We were each three or four pints deep.

"Hell of a thing happened back there," Murphy said. We'd been avoiding the topic.

"Don't worry about it," Hettinger said with a mouthful of food. Ex-military, he sat with his back straight and shoulders square, jaws chewing mechanically. "You can't be held responsible for what happened. Stupid dog."

Murphy shook his head. He was a chubby guy with a round nose, curly hair and sad eyes that always reminded me of the puppies at the pound. "Did you have to shoot the poor thing?"

Hettinger stopped chewing and nodded emphatically. "Absolutely, I did. Better than a slow death. The only humane thing to do under the circumstances. Sometimes a man's gotta make hard decisions."

Murphy didn't respond. He just shut his eyes. I was a lot closer with ol' Murph than Hettinger, who had only been hired recently and always carried a chip on his shoulder. Murphy, on the other hand, was the kind of guy who never said a cross word, and in the two years we'd worked together I'd never seen him angry. It was weird but made him hard not to like.

"That old lady sure hit the roof," I said, wondering if they'd been as creeped out by her ranting.

"I think she tried to put a spell on us," Murphy said.

"A spell? Jeez. That's funny." Hettinger chuckled and then peered over at Murphy's plate. "You gonna eat that?" When Murphy didn't answer, Hettinger forked one of his hot wings and popped it into his mouth.

I pushed away my empty plate and leaned back in the chair. I decided to focus on my beer in hope of drinking myself to sleep.

***

A thump against the door of the motel room startled my eyes open. I stared into blackness. I hadn't been sleeping, no thanks to the diesel rumble of my snoring co-workers, but I'd been trying.

At first, I dismissed the noise, probably just another drunken motel guest stumbling around outside. Then, it happened again. Like a balled fist, something gave a single heavy pounding to the door.

"You guys hear that?" I said.

No answer.

Murphy and I had drawn the short straws and had to share a bed. I looked over at Hettinger, who lay stretched out on his own. I couldn't see much beyond the green glow of a digital clock that flashed 12:01.

Hettinger snorted and rolled over. Murphy kept right on sawing logs.

Boom! There it was again—a single thud followed by a strange fluttering sound. I pictured a bird on a kamikaze mission, dive-bombing our motel room. Make that three birds. Targeting us in the middle of the night.

I rubbed my eyes and tried to compute what I was hearing, when Hettinger said, "What the hell was that?"

We waited in silence. When it didn't recur, I said, "Something was at the door."

I listened intently for any further noise outside.

The drapes parted, and Hettinger's silhouette stood at the window peering through the glass into the lighted parking lot.

"See anything?" I asked.

After a moment of further study, he said, "No. Guess it was nothing."

He reached for the drapes when—*Boom!* Something hit

the door again.

Hettinger drew the black shape of a pistol from the nightstand. His profile slipped past the window and disappeared in front of the door. He swung it open and stood with the gun aimed outside.

There was no one at the door. Nor any birds.

"What's going on?" Murphy grumbled from a tangle of sheets.

From somewhere outside, far in the distance and possibly miles away, came a deep, mournful noise. It sounded like the blare of a great horn. My skin prickled as I listened to that low, bellowing tone from a giant trumpet like some medieval call to war. I'd never heard anything like it outside a Hollywood movie.

I clicked on the bedside lamp. Hettinger looked at me. With his brow arched and lips pinched tight, he appeared worried—totally uncharacteristic.

I shrugged in return.

"What's that sound?" Murphy muttered. He sat up next to me and rubbed his face.

Hettinger lifted a finger to his mouth. "Shhhhhhhhhh," he said. "*Listen...*"

He turned around and gazed off into the darkness outside, in the direction of that eerie wail. Mixed within that menacing tone was the whisper of a gathering breeze that seemed to strengthen and swell. As the wind intensified, it stirred the drapes inside the room.

"What do you think that sound is?" Murphy said.

Hettinger shook his head. "I'm not sure I want to know."

A violent gust blasted into the room with a sudden sucking vibration. Hettinger flew from his feet. The door banged against the doorstop. My hair blew back, and my ears popped from the pressure.

Papers and beer cans swirled into the air. The clutter on

the sink counter clattered against the mirror. Toothbrushes and razors went everywhere. Murphy gave a high shout as the bedsheets pulled from his body and twisted in mid-air. I rolled from the mattress and dropped to the floor between the beds. Our clothes, overnight bags and anything untethered were scooped up by an unseen force and slung around all over.

Then it hit Hettinger. Like an invisible comet, it struck him in the gut. He folded in half and shot out the motel door, crashing into a sidewalk guardrail just outside. I jumped to my feet to help. Without a chance to catch his breath, Hettinger was hurled back into the room, as if thrown by the seat of his pants. He flew onto me, and we tumbled to the floor.

His face, inches from mine, bunched up like a baby about to burst into tears. He gasped, "What's happening to me?!"

Something ripped him off my body and rammed him against the ceiling. I rolled again. He crashed to the carpet with a shower of drywall dust.

Murphy, cursing and gibbering, pressed his back against the bed's headboard, sliding himself up the wall.

The unseen force seized Hettinger, spun him in the air and then raked him across the motel dresser, crunching him headfirst into the TV which shattered in the corner. Hettinger thrashed and jerked for freedom, but again he rose and hovered, then screamed as he soared all the way from the back of the room into the mulled front windows, which burst with shattered glass.

I saw his gun on the floor. I grabbed it. I wanted to shoot, to help, to do *anything*, but I saw nothing to shoot at.

Hettinger flew into a corner of the ceiling as if shot by a rocket. There he wiggled and gyrated and seemed to fight a seizure. His t-shirt shredded away and flew apart. Then his skin began to ripple. His face and neck swelled and pulsed in violent undulations. His flesh would sink and rise, peak and valley, and those peaks stretched higher and longer as Hettinger's growls and grunts became screams. His skin was being pulled as if snagged by fish hooks, with many lines tugging in many different directions. Those peaks pulled to the ripping point. Swaths of skin stripped away from his body. Blood sprayed in every direction. His scalp lifted away from his head like a wig torn off by a vulture. His face became a contorting mask of agony peeled away to reveal a bare skull, red and toothy but still conscious.

Good God, he's still conscious! Still screaming!

Hettinger's eyes swam madly in their sockets as his body was skinned from head to toe.

My knees turned to water. I found myself on the floor again.

Murphy dashed outside.

I needed that cue. I forced myself to my feet and stumbled out behind him. Hettinger was still gagging over my shoulder as I caught myself on the guard rail. I stared into the night sky for answers.

Murphy puked in the dead grass just a few feet away. I staggered toward him. The other guests of the hotel poked out of their rooms to investigate.

I put my hand on Murphy's shoulder. He coughed and he spat, and then lifted up with a pie-eyed look that showed the same kind of confused terror that gripped me inside.

We stood there a long time and said nothing, as a crowd gathered. Some of the people peered into our room and retched. They called the cops.

I looked down and saw Murphy had pissed his shorts. So had I.

***

The onslaught of questions came in waves that were reworded and repeated by the sheriff and his deputies countless times, over many long hours. After we'd failed to offer an explanation that satisfied the responding officers, Murphy and I were cuffed and driven to the local jail. They put us in separate holding cells, then interrogated us individually in a room alongside the main office.

We were each given a phone call. I'm sure Murphy called his wife.

I was by myself. My ex-wife Sharon had left me four months ago for an old boyfriend. She and I had been arguing lately over petty matters, but I never saw the affair coming. A real kick to the teeth.

So, I phoned the company owner, Don Morgan, a man with a lot of money who I knew would round us up a lawyer. That's exactly what he promised by the time I hung up the phone, despite my stammering inability to explain the situation. I refused to describe to him what I'd actually seen. Don was my boss, and I needed to retain credibility.

The sheriff's station was a small building with a two-desk office area and four 12-foot cells, divided into pairs by a short hallway. They kept Murphy on the other side of the hall.

I pointed out to the authorities many times, of course, that we hadn't committed a crime, but a deputy told me they could keep us on a 48-hour hold until they figured out if they should file charges.

I imagined all the investigators back at the crime scene were busy scratching their heads and vomiting into toilets.

What a mess. And I had no logical explanation for any of it.

"It was the spell." Those were the first words to leave Murphy's mouth after the deputies brought three new arrestees into the station and shuffled things around to accommodate. They locked him alone in the corner cell next to mine.

"You mean the old lady?" The thought had occurred to me, as farfetched as it seemed.

"Of course, the old lady," Murphy said with a sniffle. "The spell. Damn gypsy curse!" His eyes were red and face puffy. I hated to see him so broken down.

"You don't really believe in that stuff. Do you?"

"Not 'til last night," he said.

That was a difficult point to argue.

As much as I wanted to speak the voice of reason, to tell him that magical curses didn't exist and that the police would eventually discover a reasonable explanation for what we'd witnessed, I could not force the words. The implausibility of the whole ordeal scared the hell out of me, because it left the door open to believe what I did not want to believe: that black magic existed, that Hettinger had been targeted by a vengeful hex, and that if I remembered the old lady's ranting correctly, then Murphy and I might be next on the chopping block.

"Three nights, three bites. Isn't that what she told us?" Murphy said.

I thought for a moment, trying to misremember, trying to reinterpret what I know I had heard. "Something along those lines."

"Those were her exact words," Murphy said. "She cursed us, and it came true. Hettinger got the first bite on the first night. Now, we're goners. We're *next*."

I scanned the place. We'd been there all day, and I noticed that at least two officers always remained on duty, with others coming and going. "We're in a police station," I told him, "Surrounded by cops with guns. Seems like a pretty secure place."

Murphy blew through his teeth and shook his head. "That don't matter. You know that. You saw it. There's nothing going to stop that thing—whatever it is—from getting what it wants."

Again, it was tough to argue. I wished he'd stop doing that.

We got word that Don's lawyer had been in touch with the sheriff's office. The authorities would now have to turn us loose after 24 hours of initial detainment—or 5:35 am—if they weren't going to book us, but we'd still be stuck in jail for the night. Maybe Murphy was right about the cops being unable to protect us, but where could you run to escape this ... this *thing*?

For the longest time, Murphy laid in the next cell whimpering about never again seeing his wife and kids—two little girls, six and eight years old. And he swore that after what we experienced last night it would be impossible for him to ever sleep again. But he was wrong. He eventually started snoring.

I laid on the cot and covered my ears with a lumpy jailhouse pillow, wondering who was next on the hit list—him or me? The clock on the office wall pointed its hands at 10:15. I stared at the ceiling and listened to my heart pound like a speed bag punched by a boxer. I, too, felt like I might never sleep again.

***

I opened my eyes to the thundering tone of a distant war horn. The monstrous sound seemed to come from every direction, from above and below, growing louder and louder. It penetrated the building and echoed between the walls with escalating volume.

Murphy sat up and pulled the sheet to his chin.

A young deputy lifted his head from his desk and looked around.

"That noise," I told the deputy. "That's what we heard last night. Right before what happened to Hettinger."

I glanced at the clock—12:01.

Another cop with gray hair rushed out of the bathroom. "What the hell's that noise?"

"Beats me," the young guy said.

"I told you… it's coming!" I shouted at him. "The thing that killed our co-worker last night—it's coming *here!*"

Both officers looked at me, then at each other.

"What are you talking about?" said the young one, squinting his eyes in disbelief.

What a dunce this kid was. "The fucking *whammy!*"

The double doors to the station exploded open. A violent wind blasted inside. Every loose item swirled into a tempest of airborne clutter—paperwork, pens, hats, jackets. The young officer leapt to his feet and was instantly knocked backward. Both cops took cover behind their desks as debris ricocheted off the walls and ceiling.

The maddening noise of that ox-horn trumpet grew impossibly loud and shook me to the bowels. There was nowhere to run—trapped like a mouse cornered by a cat. Pure panic hit me in a flood. I shook the cell door, trying to break it open. It rattled on its hinges but refused to give.

"I don't want to *die!*" Murphy shrieked. "The dog was an *accident!*"

Through all the chaos, I heard a new sound, a sharp squeak that grew into a squeal. It came from the steel bars of Murphy's cell. The metal was bending, bowing apart to form a passage through the front wall. With a *CRACK!* and *SNAP!* two of the bars broke and curled into the cell. Murphy sat quaking all over, watching it happen with his mouth moving fast to form words that I could not hear. He crossed his heart over and over, and I realized he was praying.

"Murphy!" I yelled as his body shot backward and

slapped against the block wall of the cell.

He moaned as he slid up to the ceiling, then banged to the floor, then he was smeared across the wall diagonally like a rag wiping a window. With a mighty crash, he clanged against the bars that separated our cells, cutting his face on impact. He reached through the bars, grasping for me, and I lunged for his hand. He flew away again.

Hurling backward, Murphy crushed into the cement walls that formed the rear corner of the cell. Defiant of gravity, he rocketed back in my direction, raising his arms to absorb the blow. The bones crunched against the bars. Back in motion he flew to the far wall and smacked it like a bug.

"Do something!" I screamed to anyone.

Murphy soared back my direction with his shattered arms flailing like rope ladders. Again, he smashed into the bars, pulverizing him. Back to the far wall he went with a wet slap, then he soared again into the dividing bars, and a splash of blood struck my face.

The poor guy was losing all shape, parts of him flying off, pieces landing on me and around me. Again and again, his body was pounded from one side of the cell to the other, again, again. I stood there frozen and trapped. And every time his body got smashed against those unforgiving bars between us, I could not help but think a sick thought: *strain the pasta through a colander ... strain the pasta through a colander.*

That's all I remember.

***

I woke to a slap of my face—the sheriff trying to revive me. I was still in the jail cell. Blood painted everything. He and a deputy stood me up and carried me by the shoulders while I tried to remember how my legs worked. We stepped into the night, which flashed a patriotic red, white and blue from the squad of emergency vehicles on the scene.

"Can you hear me? Are you hurt?" the sheriff said.

Paramedics and police swarmed the area.

"What did you see?" he asked.

"Nothing," I managed to say. "Just like last night. I couldn't see a thing."

The two men sat me on a curb outside and returned to the station.

I sat for the longest time as people milled around me in the night, trying to explain the unexplainable. When a news crew pulled onto the scene, I got up and flagged a deputy to collect my wallet, phone and the keys to the van. It was parked around back.

Lucky me.

***

I left the scene with the smell of blood still fresh in my nose. At a nearby Waffle House, I ordered hash browns, smothered and covered, then stared at them as they turned cold. I could not seem to focus my thoughts or put a plan together. My brain had taken a beating, and exhaustion strengthened the force of gravity. After paying for the untouched plate of food, I wandered back out to the van, pulled to a corner of the lot, crawled into the back and laid down.

I woke up with a bitter taste in my mouth. Still dark outside. My phone read 9:47 pm. I'd just spent my last day on earth asleep in the back of the company van.

A stew of ugly emotions gurgled inside me. Part of it was a genuine fear for my life; another part, a deep sadness for poor ol' Murph. I also felt an antagonizing sense of helplessness—that I failed to help Hettinger, that I couldn't protect Murphy, and that I didn't know how to save myself.

"Damn gypsy curse!" Murphy had said.

Gypsy curse, my ass. Gypsies are always on the move. It occurred to me that the old lady who'd sicced the whammy on us lived in that little backwoods slum about fifteen miles off the Trapper Valley exit.

And the circumstances of the last two nights had changed considerably. Hettinger fell to a surprise attack, practically a bolt from the blue. Murphy was stuck in a jail cell, helpless but to wait for the axe to fall. But I was a free man, and I knew what was coming.

I also knew right where our problems originated.

*****

A ruddy-looking man with tobacco in his jaw opened the door of the shabby little house. I recognized him.

"I help ya?"

"I'm looking for the old lady."

"What old lady?" He looked over my shoulder suspiciously then spat black liquid into the yard. "Ain't no old lady live here."

I studied his face but didn't see much light in his eyes. "The old lady whose dog got killed."

He shot me a look and squinted. "Oh," he said. "Elnora. Wait. No. No, you can't be here." His suspicions must have grown, the way his head began to swivel back and forth, searching outside—for what I don't know.

"You been marked," the man said. "I don't want nothing to do with you."

"I know I've been marked. That's why I'm looking for her. Go get her."

"She don't live here! She was givin' my wife a readin' that day! And she ain't gonna do nothing good for you if you find her. You done killed the bee charmer's best dog. What the hell'd you think was gonna happen?"

"Bee charmer?"

"Yeah, she's a medicine lady. She probably coulda healed the dog you hadn't shot it."

Damn Hettinger and his itchy trigger-finger...

"She cursed us," I told him. "That day out here on the road. She put a hex on us."

"Not right then, she didn't," he said. "She just marked you. She must've cursed you later. And that's even worse than being marked! It's an old practice. Old as these hills, and Elnora's got roots around here deeper than the big black oaks. You should not a crossed that ol' lady."

"I *didn't*. I was in the wrong place at the wrong time. Now two of my friends are dead. I got the feeling I'm next."

The man ran his hands through his greasy salt-and-pepper hair. "I'm sorry about that, mister, but I can't help you. My wife's real sick, and I can't invite trouble over here no ways. I can't get involved."

"Where can I find the lady?"

He took a step back and pushed the door. I slapped my hand against it. "I said *where can I find her?*"

He looked at me and saw that I was a desperate man. Maybe desperate enough to be dangerous. He told me directions.

I followed them.

***

At least Mom seemed to be doing well.

"...You know how your Aunt Betty can be," she said into the phone. "I swear, if she doesn't fill her daily quota of things to complain about, then she must not feel complete as a person. So, after a while I just tune her out. I hate to be that way, but she's just too full of negativity, and I've got enough of that in my life just trying to keep your father straightened out."

The late stages of Alzheimer's had crippled my father's mind. He no longer recognized me. His memory of me was of a 5-year-old boy, a child he asked about sometimes but would never find again.

"I know you do, Mom," I told her. "You're a saint for all you do."

"Will you be coming over to see us this weekend?"

I swallowed the lump in my throat. "I'll try. I promise." My voice cracked, and she heard it.

"Are you sure everything's okay, son? You sound a little blue. Is anything wrong?"

I bit my lip and tried to regain composure. "I'm fine. Just been a long week at work, I guess. A little tired but I'll be okay. Hopefully I'll see you soon."

"Okay. I look forward to it."

"I love you. Tell Dad I love him too." My dad's refusal to talk to me was a real punch in the gut. On my last day alive, the old man knew me as a stranger.

"I will, dear. I love you. You get some rest, okay?"

"Okay. Goodbye, Mom."

I kept my ear to the phone, but the line went dead. A million memories washed over me: a piggyback ride from Dad, a hug from Mom after my first broken heart, the walks we all took together with our old dog Rascal. I'd had a good life growing up, and if I'd had the time, I would have broken down and cried like a baby.

But the phone's screen read 11:45 pm.

May the midnight clock start ticking.

I looked out the van window at the leaning two-story house on the moonlit hill where the medicine lady was said to live. A white fence with leaning pickets surrounded the place, and hanging from those pickets were strange charms and trinkets, some with metal and gems, and others made from bone. Animal skins were stretched tight and fastened to the front wall of the house beneath the rusty porch roof, and an orange glow of lamplight bled through the heavy drapes of the front window.

I shoved a hammer from the van's toolbox into the back of my jeans. Then I hopped the fence. The rickety steps of the porch creaked beneath my feet. The screen was missing from the lopsided storm door, so I reached through and knocked on the wood.

A rustling came from within and then nothing. After a moment, I knocked again.

"Who is it?" asked a craggy voice from the other side of the door.

I told her my name. I tried to apologize for the accident—even offered to buy her a new dog.

"I am genuinely sorry, ma'am. But I did not kill your dog. I was not driving the vehicle, nor did I shoot the poor thing. That was my idiot co-worker. Ma'am, I am *not* responsible and I *do not deserve to die!*" I pleaded through the closed door.

She cracked it open. An ancient face carved with wrinkles peered outside. Her eyes were deep and dark as a barred owl's, and a strange herbal aroma wafted from the house.

"You didn't drive the vehicle?" she asked.

"No, ma'am. I did not." I put my hand on my heart in a pledge of honor.

She looked down the hill. "Then what the hell is *that?*"

I turned around to see the van I'd driven there—the one that killed her pet.

"Sandy was my oldest friend, and you killed her, you sonofabitch!" She slammed the door.

I did not want to fight an old lady, but I did not want to

be torn to pieces by some invisible being.

"Call it off!" I screamed at the door. "Call off the curse!"

"Go away!" I heard from within.

My phone read 11:56.

I saw red and turned the knob. Locked. My shoulder rammed the door, which bowed inward but held. With another blow I heard the crack of splintering wood. I took a step backward, then swept forward with the other leg. The kick struck squarely next to the latch, and the door swung open with a bang.

Lit candles cast a warm glow throughout the room. Stacks of books, plates of rolled herbs, and animals frozen in taxidermy crowded the house. The old lady was loading a rifle in the corner.

I stormed her. She screamed when I grabbed the barrel, and darted her head at me, snapping her rotten teeth like a striking snake. I clutched the gun and ripped it away.

Then, in the distance, I heard it. That damn low note of death on the march, blown from a trumpet by a warrior in hell. My skin prickled all over.

"Call it off!" I screamed at the old lady.

She shook her head.

"I said call it *off*!"

The volume of that infernal noise grew by the second. The glass in the windows began to tremble. The floor vibrated beneath my feet. That *thing* was coming fast.

The old lady backed into a staircase, then turned and scampered up the steps with surprising speed. I chased up after her, tried to snatch her ragged gown and missed.

At the landing, she fled around a banister and lunged into a room. The door swung at me, but I jammed a foot at the base and wedged it open. I shoved my body against it, overpowered her and threw open the door as she careened backward.

A roaring crash sounded from downstairs. The entire house quaked and rumbled, with glassware and knickknacks shimmying on the room's dresser.

"Call it off!" I demanded.

"Never!" she snarled.

That evil bitch. I pulled out the hammer and stalked toward her. "If I've got to kill you to stop this thing, then I'll do what I have to do."

She cocked her head. Her nostrils flared. "You ain't got the guts!"

With the hammer raised, its shadow fell over Elnora's frail form; I hated to do it, but this was the only way. She backed against a second-story window, her face etched with a sneer, defiant of what I had in store for her.

But she was right. I locked up. I couldn't swing the hammer. This was not the man I wanted to be: killer of elderly women. Her skin so thin, her bones so weak. The hammer, so crushing and brutal. That most despicable sin, murder, did not seem to be in my wheelhouse.

Elnora's robe and hair swirled in a cold gust of wind. Time had run out. With explosive racket, two balusters from the stairwell flew into the room with a shower of splinters. The casing around the door tore off the walls as the thing entered with a deafening howl. The air around us whirled with flying clutter.

Terror hit me like lightning. If I was going down, so was the old lady. I grabbed the woman, pulled her close, spun her in front of me, shielding me from that damned *thing*.

And it came with a fury. I could not see it but I knew it was bearing down, licking its chops, savoring the meal. On instinct, I thrust out my arm stiffly in front of us both, knowing the thing could go right through her. My fingertips flew apart as though jammed in a fan blade. We both left our feet, everything in motion. The back of my head shattered the window. The night sky loomed down, the stars fiery bright. With no floor beneath us, we flew together, Elnora and I.

In a sudden impulse, I twisted. I shoved the screaming woman beneath me as we fell, and then *SMACK!*

***

With the rough itch of grass beneath my face, I batted my eyes open. I must've been knocked cold. The world swam around me. I remembered I should be fearing a hellish death, but ... that monstrous noise was gone. The wind had settled. I rolled off a lump beneath me and discovered a human form.

The old lady, sprawled awkwardly on the ground, did not move. My body had crushed her on impact after we'd been thrown through the upstairs window.

My hand suddenly felt engulfed in flame. I lifted my left arm to see it shorn of four fingers. The scream that tore out of my lungs hurt my own ears.

I gathered myself and limped to the steps of the house. There, I ripped off my flannel and proceeded to tear it into strips and wrap my ruined hand using my teeth. No hope in reattachment, my fingers had flown off in bits and pieces, shredded by the *thing*. Yet I was a lucky man because I had lived. A newly handicapped lucky man.

My hand ached and my head pounded as I staggered for the van.

Then, a wheezing cough came from behind me. And with it, relief. I turned to see Elnora shakily push herself to a seated position.

Her death would not haunt my conscience.

I stepped toward her, meaning to help the old lady to her feet. She whispered as I approached. No, not a whisper. Elnora was hissing under her breath, and a chill crept up my spine. I drew back.

"What'd you say?" I asked her.

She wobbled into an upright position, her entire frame heaving to catch her breath.

"What did you say just now?" I repeated.

She leveled me with her icy stare. "I said you've really gone and done it now."

"What do you mean?"

"I mean you attacking me, boy ... that's really gonna cost you." She grinned through the shadows. "That's gonna be a double whammy!" she said. "*A double whammy!*"

Those words were a chop to the throat.

She cackled madly, and the shrill sound of that wicked laugh gave rise to the faraway call of a great war trumpet, somewhere to the West—or was it East? A stiff breeze stirred around us, and all the warmth drained straight out of me.

That did it…

Every man's got his limitations.

Amongst the shards of glass and wood fragments, the hammer I'd found in the van gleamed on the ground in the pale moonlight. I bent down in the gathering wind and grabbed it. I gained an instant appreciation for its weight and hardness.

"Just what do you think you're gonna do with *that?*" croaked the old lady.

I tightened my grip on the handle. "Come here and I'll show you."

This bitch was going down.

The End

Men of Their Word

For the first time ever, I found myself disappointed in my father. It hurt to admit this, but the way he had surrendered to such a grave injustice struck me as downright weak. I'd never considered my father a weak man, but he'd placed his bet on a legal system that had failed him, failed my sister, failed us all. We now had every right to seek our own brand of justice. Instead, my father went reclusive, shut me out, and began spending every minute tinkering in his workshop.

Pathetic.

The whole ordeal began two years ago with the screams of Ellie May. I heard her voice in the distance, and slid my creeper from under the Bobcat where I'd been wrestling with a leaky hydraulic hose. I saw my sister staggering out of the thicket wearing nothing but a torn t-shirt with red stains. One look at her knocked the breath out of me. Poor Ellie, so delicate and innocent.

I raced across the field straight for her, as bombs exploded inside my head. *Boom!* The blood stains meant she'd been hurt. *Boom!* She's naked so she'd probably been attacked. *Boom!* She's running from the direction of the neighboring farm, which means that sicko Herbert Hayden probably had a hand in whatever had happened.

By the time I drew near, I saw she'd been beaten too. She tumbled right into my arms so bruised and broken that she'd never be the same, and I cried with her.

Never the same, my sweet little sis.

She curled in on herself from that day forward, although we did get her to acknowledge that Herbert Hayden, the local cat-torturing creep and known peeping tom, had in fact committed the assault.

Oh, how I hated that bastard, and prayed that God would send one of those explosions to blow Herbert Hayden into a million bits and pieces. *Boom!*

***

The court found Herbert Hayden guilty as charged, but by the time the trial had concluded, that gawky, pimple-faced little shit ended up serving only six months in a juvenile detention center. He'd been a minor at the time of the crime, which qualified him as a juvenile offender according to the penal code. On his eighteenth birthday, the state was forced to turn him loose.

Ellie May had suffered three cracked ribs, two black eyes, a broken nose, and the loss of her purity at the hands of Herbert Hayden, yet he'd only served a short vacation for his crimes.

Ellie May, on the other hand, would not speak. She refused to eat. She began to cut herself.

One rainy afternoon, I walked upstairs having made her a sandwich. The peanut-butter-and-banana with no crusts had once been her favorite, and while I knew it would be a long shot, it would do us all good if she'd eat something. No surprise that she did not answer my knock on the door. I slipped inside, backing into the room with the plate in hand, and pulled the door closed behind me. Something bumped my shoulder.

I turned to find Ellie May hanging there, her lifeless eyes wide open and drying out. A noose from the ceiling fan had squeezed all the color from her face. I dropped the plate and fell to my knees.

As far as I was concerned, Herbert Hayden was guilty of murder — a crime for which he had not served a single day. He deserved to die.

And soon, I felt the same about the elder Mr. Hayden.

***

After that, we had the dust-up at the hardware store. It's inevitable to happen in such a small town. Arch enemies are bound to cross paths. Tempers flare.

You couldn't really blame my dad for what happened. He had always been an old soul, a humble and soft-spoken farmer with a stiff upper lip, calloused hands and the dependable character of the men who built this fine country. He found his morality in the Word of God, and his faith ran deep. But, they say "to err is human and to forgive is divine." That means my dad was only human, and only God forgives.

Dad and I had stopped by the store for a few supplies. He needed welding rods. I needed toggle bolts. We were perusing the tool aisle when he caught sight of Herbert Hayden. Dad's face went blank.

All gangly and slouching, Herbert hunkered in a corner of the store while holding his phone up close to his greasy eyeglasses. I followed his aim to a young girl in pigtails and short-shorts who stood in the cashier line with her mother. I didn't have to see Herbert's screen to know he was recording her on video.

Dad must have realized the same thing, because his blank expression went blood red and twisted into a war mask. Before I could react, he torpedoed down the aisle and lunged for the asshole's throat. Dad grabbed him by the neck with both fists and squeezed. Herbert's glasses fell off, his eyes bugged out, and at that moment I filled up with a kind of righteous glee.

I wish I hadn't, though, because in that instance of satisfaction, I dropped my guard. I should have maintained what police officers call "situational awareness." Then, I would have seen Barnaby Hayden step out of the gardening aisle with a shovel. He swung it wide, and the flat of the blade ding-donged Dad right on top of the scalp. Knocked him cold. I caught Dad before he hit the floor, brought him to a rest, and then I charged Old Man Hayden.

I managed to belt him hard across the cheek before the staff of the hardware store latched onto us both to tear us away from each other.

I wanted the man's blood. I could practically taste it — his and his son's dripping right off my tongue.

"I want to kill them both," I told Dad afterward.

"I don't blame you," he answered.

"The court turned him loose," I said. "After what he did to Ellie, they still turned him loose. That's not right. It's not fair. It's not justice."

"God will judge them," he said. "They can't escape that."

What he was saying left me hollow. I told him, "I don't have time to wait for God."

Ever since that day, Dad had been pulling his hermit act, hiding in his work shed. I could hear the hammering. I'd see the shop glow bright with the loud buzzing of arc-welds. He was burying himself in some sort of work, but not the work that we needed to do.

Me, on the other hand ... I'm no hermit.

***

The clouds gathered thick and black in late afternoon. I drove past Dad outside his work-shed when I headed to our back acreage. His tailgate hung open as he rolled a large black disc out of the bed of his pickup. Was that a manhole cover? I'd seen him unloading some curious items lately ... a new anvil ... something that looked like the torsion spring of a garage door. I might have asked what he was working on if I hadn't been so angry with him.

Besides, I had some curious cargo of my own. Herbert Hayden lay bound and gagged in the back of my Cherokee. Our family's deer shack stood hidden back deep on our property, and I had big plans to go out there and make this monster scream.

And scream he did.

***

At first, our time together didn't come easy, but I was determined to hear Herbert give me a reason why he'd done what he did. See, Ellie had had one those conditions that made her halfway mute, timid as a mouse, and scared of her own shadow. How could he hurt such a fragile creature? Well, he wouldn't speak up when I asked him, so I gave him some encouragement. And when he still wouldn't tell me why, I lost my temper.

After an hour or two, I had plum tuckered myself out while breaking Herbert's bones.

His hands had become strange sea crustaceans, pink and blue pulpy things that quivered in pain. My sledgehammer had snapped the wood of the chair beneath his left wrist, and that forearm drooped like a dishrag from its midpoint since both bones had been pulverized. The other chair arm broke further toward the back, and that blow had sent bone shards jutting out of Herbert's skin. When that happened—boy, how he went to howling about being sorry for what he'd done. Seeing the white of your own bones will do that to a fella.

Unfortunately for him, his lesson in our hunting shack had yet to end.

I did a thorough job on his left leg. My goal was to completely obliterate the bone structure, and a 20-lb. steel sledgehammer will do the trick. When I started on the right one, I intended to flatten his foot into a cartoon-like pancake shape, and while that didn't exactly happen, the only way Herbert will ever remove that foot from his Converse is if he pours it out like a bowl of soup.

I then smashed his shin in half with a single mighty blow. The right leg now had two knees.

I caught my breath while Herbert sat strapped to the chair hyperventilating.

"Here's the deal," I told him. "You're going to tell me one more time exactly why you attacked my poor baby sister. My little sister who couldn't live with herself after what you did. My poor little sister, who you killed whether you want to admit it or not. You're going to tell me once more why you did it, and if you do, then I will not kill you today. If you don't, then I'm going to break open your skull right here and now. Do you understand?"

Herbert grunted something through clenched teeth, but I knew he had gotten the message. We had rehearsed this several times.

"I'm a sick piece of shit," he sputtered. But he kept going. "I could never get a girl on my own because I'm a worm, not a man. I'm a lowlife, worthless slime and I don't deserve to live. I did it because I am an evil coward."

He gasped out the last word, the end of the prepared little speech which I made him memorize.

"Fair enough," I said. "I'm a man of my word." I hoisted the sledgehammer high over my shoulder then chopped it down and splintered his kneecap.

He roared. I smiled. Ol' Noodle-legs, they'll call him.

I used my buck knife to cut the twine that bound him. He spilled out of the chair into a pile on the floor. With no bones in his arms or legs, he'd have a fine time crawling to safety.

"I'm going home," I told him. "Beware the wolves, asshole."

That's when I heard it: *"Herbert, are you in there?"*

That voice from outside the deer shack, I recognized. Old Man Hayden had joined us.

I also heard something else approaching in the distance. It sounded like an engine. I tightened my grip on the knife.

When I let the door swing open, Barnaby Hayden stood outside with his shotgun aimed right at me. He had one of those ancient faces like he'd been chipped out of stone, and right then he looked harder than ever.

"I heard my boy hollering," the man said. "I know my son's voice. What the hell did you do to him?"

"Daddy?" Herbert moaned from behind me.

"Herbie! You okay in there?"

The engine I heard had been our Bobcat loader. My dad sat in the operator chair, rambling the old skid-steer across the field in our direction. From the look of the machine, Dad had given it some sort of custom modifications.

"He hurt me, Daddy. Real bad."

Barnaby glared at me like a hawk at a hare. "You rotten sumbitch."

I eased myself down the stacked concrete blocks that served as the two makeshift steps of the shack. "You know exactly what your scumbag son did to my sister…"

The Bobcat bounded over a couple of deep ruts then bounced to a stop just a couple feet shy of Barnaby, who cast a glance at Dad's growling machine but kept the two-barrel muzzle pointed at me.

Herbert wallowed to the edge of the doorway and poked out his head. "Daddy..."

Barnaby Hayden racked his shotgun and leveled it at my face. "What did you do to my boy?"

"My sister killed herself because of what he did to her."

Barnaby's nostrils flared. "She got what she had coming. She knew what she was looking for, when she wandered onto my property. My boy just gave her what she wanted."

That's when my father finally spoke up.

"Mr. Hayden..." he said.

The man turned the shotgun on my dad and raised it eye level. He did not say a word, but my father did.

"...It seems that you've now wandered onto *my* property," Dad told him while flipping a lever I did not recognize on the side of the Bobcat.

The Bobcat screeched and hissed, then sounded a loud pop as the wheels bucked. In a blur of metal, a huge steel armature snapped from the rear over the cabin. Something struck the ground with such heavy force the vibration shook my feet. Suddenly, blood covered my father, the Bobcat, the shack, and my face.

Barnaby Hayden had vanished. On the ground in front of the Bobcat, alongside a huge mass of black iron, I saw a boot, a hand, some crumpled denin, but the old man had been smashed into a splash, the fallout of which I could still hear landing in the straw grass all around us. *Boom!*

Herbert made some sort of mewling noise from the doorway of the deer shack.

It took a moment for me to register what had whipped over the Bobcat carried by a chassis of steel I-beams and coil springs. The business end of the weapon had been forged using a large anvil welded to a sewer cover, with its trigger apparatus driven by a combination of hydraulics and mechanical torsion. A farmer's ingenuity.

Crudely engraved on the anvil were three little words that explained a lot about my old man and put to rest many of my doubts. He'd carved "Hammer of God" into the side of his invention, and at that moment I'd never been prouder to be his son.

We both dragged Herbert Hayden out of the shack, and I let Dad do the honors of hammering that bastard into nothing.

Herbert had a price to pay, but I am indeed a man of my word.

The End

To Kill a Guy Twice

"So, you've actually seen the ghost? No kidding?"

"No kidding," Jimmy Miller replied to his new friend and neighbor Eric Hyde, who was carving his initials into the treehouse wall. "I saw it. I wish I could *un*-see it."

A rumble of distant thunder grew to a booming quake like a giant boulder rolling overhead. The two had climbed into Eric's plywood shack an hour ago to play cards and read comics. Then a heavy rain fell, and they decided to wait out the downpour rather than shimmy down the rope ladder and get soaked on the thirty-yard dash to the house. While twiddling away the time, Eric asked the crucial question: *You ever seen the ghost of Caleb Wilder?*

"What'd it look like? Were you scared?" Eric pressed, his eyes narrowing in genuine intrigue. He had dark, curly hair and liked to dress in camouflage and army green every day of the week. The two boys had become fast friends after Jimmy moved to the street and they'd first met each other in the woods, where they'd each ventured to hunt squirrels with BB guns. Neither had yet to bag a squirrel.

"Yeah, I was scared." Jimmy admitted, knowing full well how uncool it sounded for a 14-year-old to say. "You'd have been scared, too."

Jimmy's parents had purchased the old house across the street for what his father described as a "steal." The family had to relocate from Georgia when he'd been transferred by his job. They planned to remodel the old two-story home, structurally sound but cosmetically dated, and put down roots in Trapper Valley, a seemingly quiet suburb just north of Birmingham, Alabama.

Not until after moving in did Jimmy learn why the house had remained unoccupied at such an inviting price: The locals believed it to be haunted.

Eric sheathed the survival knife he'd been using to etch his mark in the wood. "Well, what did it look like? A skeleton? All guts and eyeballs?"

Jimmy told him that initially the ghost appeared as only a shape, a shadow that should not have been where it was. He had crept into the kitchen late one Friday night, his first week in the house. His parents had retired to their bedroom, and he'd fallen asleep watching a *Friday the 13th* sequel, awaking after midnight with a hunger. Jimmy snagged a plastic-wrapped cupcake from the pantry and opened the refrigerator, its white light spilling into the darkness. As he rummaged for the milk, he felt a looming presence behind him.

He spun with jug in hand and scoured the room. The single fridge bulb illuminated the kitchen, but the living area on the far side of the countertop island remained murky. Shipping crates and stacks of cardboard boxes cluttered the room, but he saw no one or no *thing* watching him.

Until it moved.

Jimmy's breath caught in his throat. The dull glare of moonlight bled through a window, and along its edge he saw motion. Something black and opaque flashed across the gray square of the sky and then vanished into the opposite corner of the room.

Jimmy's first thought: *burglar*. His second: *the ghost*. His fingers tightened on the cold, sweaty handle of the milk jug. Had it been a trick of the light? Maybe an owl flew past the window…

He craned his neck for a better view, but kept his feet planted ready to dash up the staircase and scream for help. Focusing his gaze beyond the reach of the fridge light, the darkness gained contrast, and Jimmy felt eyes on him. He took a single stride into the living room and made out a figure in the corner. An arm, a leg, a torso—Jimmy's bladder quivered. When a gasp escaped him, the figure shifted in his direction, turning a pale face toward him, and Jimmy bolted.

Stumbling over his feet, he tripped forward, caught himself on the counter, milk jug pounding down onto the floor and sliding to the stove. He twisted around and dashed to the stairwell, slapping the wall for the light switch. The chandelier blazed to life, and Jimmy saw it all: coffee table, sofa, storage boxes, and his own harried reflection in the corner window. Nothing else occupied the room. Jimmy was alone.

"At first I think he was only watching me," Jimmy said. "He wanted to scope out the newcomers, see what he had to deal with."

Eric weighed this and nodded. "Makes sense. If I was haunting a house, I'd want to know who was moving in."

"That's how it began, anyway. Then he started getting aggressive."

"Aggressive?"

"Yeah. Like he wanted to scare me away."

Eric curled a smile. "Scare you away? Like *booga-booga?*" He gave a snigger.

"Fine," Jimmy said. "I won't tell you."

A gust of wind howled through a broken window, spitting cold rain on Jimmy's arm, giving him goose-bumps.

Eric reached up and unhooked a loop of twine that attached a thin wooden door to a hook on the ceiling. Hinged at the top, the door swung down and snapped over the window. He leaned back against the wall and opened a

Punisher comic, thumbing through the pages and skimming the artwork.

"Go on," Eric said. "So, Caleb Wilder's ghost got 'aggressive' with you... What'd he do? You know he was a pretty sick puppy, right? That's how he ended up in his current condition—*dead*."

"All Mom and Dad told me is that he died under mysterious circumstances, so the locals made up a story about a ghost."

Eric sat up as his eyes widened. "Wait. You mean you don't even know the story of what happened in your house? I guess nobody wanted to tell your parents. Either that, or they are giving you a seriously whitewashed version of events. Because there ain't *no* mystery about how he died. Everybody knows exactly what happened."

"How? Were you there?"

"No. Of course not. But I know the story of Jesus and Mary and Joseph, and I wasn't there either."

"So..." Jimmy said, "tell me what happened."

Eric cracked his knuckles and folded his legs beneath him Indian-style. "Well, it happened a long time ago. And the first thing you've got to realize is that Caleb Wilder was a real grade-A scumbag."

By "scumbag," Eric meant he was devoid of any redeeming qualities whatsoever, just like Caleb's mother and father. Jimmy thought that was a hefty claim to make of even the rottenest human beings, but didn't bother to argue.

Eric told him Old Lady Wilder, a notorious loud-mouthed alcoholic, could clear a room with her acrid breath, and Caleb's dim-witted dad had been confined to the St. Clair Correctional Facility for armed robbery. Every Wilder in town had a reputation as conniving, deceitful and mean as a hornet, and the whole family wore that hate like a badge of honor. By the age of seventeen, Caleb had adopted the family tradition of drunken carousing and became a regular occupant of the city jail, picked up on all manner of charges.

And, whereas cruelty to animals today signals all sorts of warning alarms to law enforcement about a person's psychotic tendencies, that particular behavioral association wasn't as clear-cut decades ago. Caleb had been caught gutting a neighborhood cat. After a few days in jail, the authorities let him back on the street. They would live to regret that decision.

"The guy killed a cat?" Jimmy had a tinge of sympathy for any kid growing up in such lousy circumstances as the Wilder boy, but word of animal cruelty instantly stemmed his good will.

"Worse," Eric said.

"He killed a dog?"

"Even worse."

"A person?"

Eric's lips tightened to a thin line. He looked more serious than Jimmy had ever seen him. "Persons," he whispered. "And they were kids."

A crack of thunder startled them both, and they chuckled nervously at its timing.

"Kids?" Jimmy asked as the laughter fell away.

Eric stopped smiling. "Three of them."

***

The feel of cold, dead flesh never bothered Caleb Wilder, but once the smell took hold, he would lose all interest in a corpse. He rolled the stiffened little girl off his bed. The body struck the dusty floorboards with a thud.

His brain thumped from last night's whiskey, and his stomach gurgled with acid. He rubbed the crust from his eyes, dreading the labor of digging another hole in the hard ground during the bitter winter. But the body had to be hidden. She stunk. And everyone was looking for her.

He saw movement from the corner of his eye. To his left something flitted away from the window, and he heard murmurs outside. He leapt to his feet and grabbed his jeans, hopping up and down to jam a leg inside. He jerked them up to his waist as voices rose outdoors. Caleb snatched a dirty sheet from the mattress, spread it over the corpse, and slid it beneath the bed. He turned to see a horrified face staring through the window at his crime. Then another face appeared.

"In here! It's the Wilder boy!"

"Good Lord—he's got Margie Hemmings!"

A patter of footfalls gathered outside. Caleb dashed out the room and sprinted down the hall. He'd left his pistol on the kitchen table. Glass shattered somewhere behind him. A heavy pounding echoed through the house as the people outside beat on the bolted front door. He rounded the kitchen counter and lunged for the table where he'd left the thirty-eight. The gun was missing. The back door hung ajar.

"Don't move, or I'll shoot!"

The familiar hammer-cock of his own revolver clicked right behind his ear.

Large hands clasped his arms and shoulders, shoving him to the table. His face broke an unfinished plate of three-day-old scrambled eggs. The weight of two or three men pinned him down.

He heard the front entrance splinter open. The stomp of boots shook the floor and table beneath his cheekbone. He heard the wail of a female voice, and pictured Mrs. Hemmings huddled over the remains of the child stuffed under his bed. Caleb smirked.

Unseen hands held down his head so he could see only cracks in the kitchen plaster, but several new shadows climbed the walls as a mob surrounded him.

"We oughtta blow his brains out right here."

"Nah. Hang him like the old days."

"I want to burn him alive."

"Don't you *touch* him!" hissed a wavering voice in a higher pitch than the rest. "You let me have him first!"

Two burly, bearded men ripped Caleb up and hurled him back down on his back, snapping his spine on the table ledge. He bit his lip to stop from screaming in pain—and giving these people what they wanted.

"Where's the others?" the woman sniffled. Mascara streaked down from her red, watery eyes. Caleb recognized the sharpened carving knife in her hand. He'd used it many times. "You tell me where to find those other little angels, you piece of *garbage!*"

He parted his lips, blood trickling out, and smiled. "They're mine now."

Those were the last words of Caleb Wilder. The men held his head while Mrs. Hemmings cut out his tongue. Then the others went to work on his eyes. They cut off his nose, cut off his ears—everything.

***

"'Cording to the story, everyone had a turn that day, cutting him to pieces, bit by bit," Eric said. "It happened right inside your *house*, dude."

Jimmy's mouth went dry. He gnawed his cheek to generate saliva and form a question. "Everyone? What do you mean 'everyone'?"

"Everybody who caught him with the dead girl, I guess. The search party. Everybody who was there that day participated in the execution as a kind of loyalty oath. Trapper Valley's a small town, even smaller back then, and people tended to look out for each other. The cops had already turned Wilder loose once, so the law couldn't be trusted. People saw there was a killer among them, and knew what had to be done. If everybody took part in the killing, then everybody shared the responsibility. Besides," Eric said, "what are the cops gonna do? Arrest the whole town?"

Jimmy lifted the small wooden door and looked out the saw-cut window to his house across the street. His dad had been sprucing up the inside, but the shabby exterior still suffered from grimy siding, peeling paint and a roof streaked with black algae. "You said he killed three kids. What happened to the other two?"

Eric joined him at the window. The rain had stopped falling, but a cold breeze stirred through the treehouse as they watched water drip from the eaves Jimmy's new home.

"Two girls," Eric said. "Just like little Margie Hemmings, he'd killed them both. And did things to the bodies."

"Did things?" Jimmy said. "What kind of things?"

Eric glanced at him and shrugged. "You know. *Things*." He looked at the floor. That's all he needed to say.

"Where'd they find them?"

Eric pointed outside. "Buried in shallow graves. Right in your backyard."

Jimmy swallowed thickly and decided it was high time to have a long talk with his parents.

***

"I think Eric is pulling your leg, son." Jimmy's dad forked a piece of roast beef and stuck it in his mouth.

Jimmy poked at his mashed potatoes beneath the yellow light of the dining room fixture. "The way he tells it, the whole town knows what happened to the Wilder kid. Right here in this house. Everyone knows except you guys."

His mother raised an eyebrow to his father. "David, there'd better not be any truth to this story." Her voice matched her stern glare.

"Relax, both of you," his dad said. "It didn't happen. Just a silly local legend. Pretty grisly story, sure. Karen, you don't seriously believe a mob of vigilantes cornered some killer in here and carved him like a turkey, do you?"

"Please don't be so graphic. We're having dinner."

His dad swigged down some iced tea. "Don't blame me. Your son's fault."

"Eric swore up and down it's true," Jimmy said.

"He swore that he *heard* it was true," his mother corrected.

"Right" his dad said. "He's just trying to spook you. Besides, even if it were true—which it isn't—what would be the big deal? It happened, what, twenty-thirty years ago? Doesn't mean a thing to us. I mean, what are you worried about? Ghosts?"

His dad's dismissal of the idea before he'd even introduced it told Jimmy everything he needed to know about seeking his help with the matter. If an adult were to claim to have seen a ghost, his parents would secretly roll their eyes, but also entertain the story in a polite and patient manner. If he, on the other hand, were to make the same claim then they would dismiss it completely out of hand, without a second thought. Case closed. Jimmy's just being weird.

Teenagers are only taken seriously when they've done something wrong. Jimmy was on his own.

He stared at his food, growing colder by the second. His appetite had left him, and he laid down his fork.

***

Two weeks later the house had become a tomb.

"'Night, Mom. 'Night, Dad," Jimmy said from the doorway of their room.

They both lay in bed, reading. Expressionless. Each nodded wordlessly without so much as meeting his eyes. Then he turned in.

He laid his head on his cool pillow, closed his eyes and counted sheep. It never worked to help him sleep, but picturing fluffy cartoon sheep leaping single-file over a picket fence served as a pleasant distraction from the worry that now plagued him morning, noon and night. He feared for the fate of his family.

The spirit of Caleb Wilder slithered through every crack and crevice of his new home, and visual manifestation was only one of the ways it made its presence known. Since they'd moved in, a pervasive coldness haunted the house from attic to cellar, and no matter how his dad chased it with the furnace, the chill would not relent. His father blamed a drafty crawlspace, but Jimmy knew the cause was more sinister.

His parents, traditionally a cheery couple, now laughed much less, and even casual conversation in the house had slowed to a trickle. An insulating silence seemed to leaden everyday life. Jimmy knew deep down that Caleb, lurking in the shadows, was leeching the light and love away from his family, just as he'd done to the handful of other occupants who'd formerly lived in the home.

Although Jimmy could find no proof of murder at their new address when researching online, he discovered that the house had swapped owners four times over the past two decades, and none of the families had lasted much more than a year before vacating. Their new home appeared to be a place where happiness went to die.

Jimmy hated it, but not the house itself. He knew exactly who to blame, just not what to do about it.

As he teetered on the brink of drifting off, a faint whisper, unintelligible, drifted through his bedroom like a strand of spider silk carried by a breeze. It came again, and he made out a single word—his own name. *Jimmy...*

He opened his eyes and gave a screech. An eyeless, fleshy skull hovered inches from his face. The lipless mouth stretched a hideous grin beneath the black triangle of its shorn nose. Jimmy bucked and thrashed, slapping and swatting with pure mad instinct but only batting air—the ghastly visage vanished as instantly as it had appeared.

Jimmy sat bolt upright in his bed, his breath coming in rapid puffs. He heard a trample of footsteps. The door shook with a knock.

"Jimmy, you okay?" his mother said.

"Yes, Mom. Come on in."

His mother showed a begrudging respect for his privacy and always asked permission before entering. Permission to enter, however, was permission to dote, so she rushed into the room, sat on his bedside and placed a hand on his forehead.

"What's wrong, honey?"

"Nothing," he said, pulse settling. "Just a bad dream."

She hugged him to her breast. "Oh sweetie, what are we going to do with you? This is becoming a pattern."

Jimmy took comfort in his mother's warm embrace— rare these days—as he stared into the darkest corner of his room, searching for any sign of the ghost. Caleb Wilder's favorite game was torment, and Jimmy was his new toy.

"I don't know what to do, Mom," he said. "But I'm going to figure it out."

***

Eric raised his trusty survival knife. "This is what you need."

The six-inch black blade had been forged of hardened inch-wide steel. With saw-tooth serrations along its back the thing looked capable, with a little elbow grease, of removing someone's head.

"Pop gave me this for camping," he said. "But I carry it around for self-defense. You never know... When the crap hits the fan, it's good to be prepared."

"What kind of crap?" Jimmy pulled a gummy worm from a package on the treehouse floor and slurped it up like a noodle.

"Who knows? Could be anything. Terrorists. Disgruntled postal workers. In your case, ghosts." The knife handle was hollow and capped with a ball compass, which Eric twisted off the end. "Inside this little storage compartment it's got a wire saw, a fishing hook and line— even a lead weight—plus a sewing needle in case you need to stitch yourself up." Eric retrieved these items from the handle to exhibit.

"Cool," Jimmy said, and he meant it.

"Yeah, I figure if a zombie apocalypse breaks out, I've got a pretty good leg up on the situation. And a weapon like this would be a good start when it comes to protecting your family from ... your little problem."

Jimmy's problem had worsened. Not only did the specter plague his sleepless nights, but Jimmy's family was under constant invisible attack.

Dirty dishes were piling up in the kitchen. Dust bunnies roamed freely across the floorboards. He'd run out of clean underwear, having long grown accustomed to fresh laundry magically reappearing in his chest-of-drawers. His homemaker mother now spent the majority of her days asleep in bed. When asked if she felt okay, if maybe she were sick or depressed, she brushed off the suggestion and acted as though it were a silly question.

Jimmy had become the resident dishwasher.

His father, too, had become an emotionless drone, diving into his remodeling every day after work without so much as acknowledging Jimmy or his mother's presence. Sanding, taping, priming, painting—robotically—one room and then the next. He worked with mechanical precision rarely speaking a word. And the most frustrating development was his parents' utter obliviousness to the change in their personalities and how it taxed the health and well-being of the family. They were infected with a cancer only he could detect, and Jimmy knew without a doubt that Caleb Wilder was the tumor.

"The problem is," Jimmy said. "Caleb Wilder is already dead. In fact, the people of Trapper Valley used knives, much like that one, to cut him to pieces. And he still comes back."

"So..."

"*So*," Jimmy said. "How do you kill a guy twice?"

"I'm not sure. But have you even tried?"

Whether it would kill the thing or not, sinking a big blade into the evil ghost did appeal to Jimmy on primal level. His options were limited, and he supposed it was worth a shot.

"I found instructions online for assassinating a target with a knife."

"Jeez," Jimmy said. "I guess you can find pretty much anything online."

"Reckon so." Eric stood up. He unfolded a printed sheet of paper from his pocket and handed it to Jimmy. "It describes the technique here. Basically, the target is approached from the rear. You're supposed to grasp the mouth and nose in a clamped palm and simultaneously thrust the knife into the right kidney area, withdraw the knife and slash the throat from ear to ear."

As he described the tactic, he pantomimed the procedure, executing an imaginary victim and dropping them to the treehouse floor.

"Another variation," he said, "is instead of slicing the throat, the blade is stabbed into the neck three or four inches below the ear until it protrudes from the opposite side. Then the knife is slashed outwards, through the throat." He sliced the knife out of the imaginary neck. "I've been practicing."

"Looks like it."

"Take this," Eric said, sheathing the blade and extending it handle first. "Keep in mind that this weapon is my prized possession, and I would not loan it to just anybody. But you're a good bud. And you need it."

Jimmy took the knife and gazed upon it with reverence. "Thanks, man," he said. "I'll put it to good use."

***

The night was quiet. The dim bulb of his fish tank lit the corner of his room with a dull blue glow. Lying in bed with hands behind his head, Jimmy glassed every nook and cranny of the room, trying to penetrate the darkness with eagle vision. When Caleb would appear, it was always as a slender charcoal silhouette and a bone-white face more corpse than man. Pitch black holes marked the features of his face. The apparition would often show up to jar Jimmy out of his slumber. He figured the ghost's plan was to keep him bedraggled, weary and weak—to wear him down, and then one day finish him off. But tonight Jimmy had a surprise.

Movement flickered near the fish tank, and he knew he wasn't alone. His pulse quickened.

"I know you're here," Jimmy said. "What do you want?"

He didn't understand the spirit's method of movement. On past encounters it seemed to leak from the shadows, vanish in a blink, then materialize elsewhere within the beat of a bat's wing. Jimmy's sat up in bed. His eyes danced across the room, ready to lung in any direction.

"Why not show yourself?" It took great effort for him to speak with a steady voice. Maybe antagonism would get a rise out of the thing. "What are you afraid of?"

An impulse nagged him to grab the nightstand lamp, pull the chain and awash the room with light. But a second thought told him it wouldn't work; Caleb Wilder seemed only to appear in the darkness.

A whisper tickled his ear. *What are you afraid of?*

Jimmy snatched the knife from beneath his pillow and sliced through the air. A snide chuckle came from behind him. He spun and swung out in an arc, the blade finding nothing.

Another snicker over his shoulder, and Jimmy stabbed before turning, spinning his body to follow through into black empty space. The voiceless hiss came again: *What are you afraid of?*

Jimmy knew the thing was projecting those words somehow, not speaking them. It had no tongue to form them.

"Where are you?" Jimmy stepped to the middle of the room. He crouched with the knife ready and eager. "Are you chicken? Is that why you hide?"

The shape edged into the dim blue light of the room's corner. Jimmy first saw the arm, thin and inky, then a leg. He inched toward it. The thing's scraggly hair spiked and curled around its pallid face like a crown of thorns.

Jimmy, it whispered and then laughed.

Jimmy lunged and got him this time, drove the knife dead center of its chest, but met no resistance. The blade went right through him like stabbing an illusion. Jimmy's breath seized. Standing face to butchered face, the thing drew back its mangled mouth in a grimy smile and cackled. Elbow deep, Jimmy dug the blade around futilely in its spectral body. He felt no flesh or bone, nor smelled its gory decay. But around the torn rim of Caleb Wilder's missing eyes squirmed tiny countless vermin. And deep within those black pits he faintly saw the ashen faces of three little girls, screaming in terror.

The thing's wiry hands shot up and slashed at his throat. Jimmy cried out, leapt back in panic.

He was alone.

Jimmy threw a hand to his Adam's apple, gasping, spinning around in search of the ghost. But he saw nothing. And his throat felt fine.

He let go of his neck and saw no blood on his fingers. Heart racing, he took a deep breath. He sat on the bed and clutched his head.

Calm down, he thought. *You're not hurt. You're fine. You faced it down. You walked away... Think about what just happened.*

His mind still swimming, it took several bangs on the door for him to realize his mother was knocking.

"I asked if everything was all right," his mom said. "I heard you shout."

"Uh. Yeh-*yes*, Mom," he stammered. "Sorry. Come on in."

The door opened. She went to his side, slid an arm around his shoulders, but blanched when she saw the knife.

"What's going on, son?"

He looked at the blade and put it down on the nightstand. Still foggy, he said, "Our house really is haunted, Mom. The story is true."

She squinted her eyes.

"It's okay, though," he said. "Because I realized something tonight. The ghost can't really hurt us. I can't seem to harm him, but he can't touch us either. And if he can't hurt me, then there's really nothing to be afraid of."

Jimmy spoke the next words louder so Caleb Wilder might hear: "I guess when it gets right down to it, a ghost is really just a *wimp*. Nothing to it. Nothing but a stupid little *nuisance!*" He swept the room with glance, inspecting the shadows, unsure where to aim his fury.

Jimmy's dad appeared in the doorway. "Everything okay?" Those were the first words he'd heard his old man speak in days.

His mother looked at Jimmy, then at his dad, shaking her head. "Don't worry. Jimmy's just being weird."

***

The incident with the knife had eliminated half of Jimmy's problem—the corpselike-phantom-terrorizing-him portion of the haunting. While technically a failure at dispatching the thing, the face-to-face confrontation proved the ghost of Caleb Wilder was all but fangless, relying on fear and intimidation. Jimmy had not only shed his fear of bodily harm but now kindled a righteous rage against what he saw as his arch nemesis.

Its presence continued to poison his home. His parents remained stuck in an emotionless mire, zombie-walking through life with nothing to jump-start their personalities short of the fearful nighttime screams of their son. And those days were over.

"Too bad the knife didn't work," Eric said over the phone.

"It didn't kill him," Jimmy said. "But now I know Caleb can't kill me, either. That is crucial information."

"I'd say so."

"Now it's time for phase two."

"What do you mean?"

"For my parents' sake, I've got to get rid of the ghost completely."

"Phase two," Eric said. "Total eradication. Awesome. What's the plan?"

"I'm not sure. I was thinking maybe some sort of spell. Maybe even an exorcism."

"I'm in. But what do you know about exorcisms?"

"Nothing," Jimmy said. "But I'm willing to learn. Feel like going to the bookstore? I need to give your knife back, anyway."

"That's cool. I'll meet you out on the street."

Saturday afternoon brought a clear sky and a pleasant breeze. A few blocks beyond their neighborhood, a small business district included a couple of fast-food joints, a bank, post office and Burnside Books—Jimmy's favorite local shop.

Waiting for Eric to join him roadside, he opened the mailbox. Jimmy tucked the survival knife beneath his arm and sorted through the letters, hoping in vain for something interesting with his name on it. A car whizzed by as he filed through the stack. He found only bills and advertisement circulars for "unbelievable markdowns" on new vehicles.

As he stuffed the mail back in the box, a familiar sense of unease fell over him like a cold rain. Jimmy looked around. At first, nothing appeared out of the ordinary. A station wagon cruised past without incident. Two blackbirds took flight from a power line and soared into the sky. He noticed Eric had left his front porch and was walking across the lawn toward the street. Jimmy saw nobody else, but then heard a reptilian whisper behind him.

What are you afraid of?

Jimmy spun to see Caleb Wilder's skeletal figure ten yards away on his porch, with his white face cocked at an angle. Jimmy lost his breath. He blinked twice, hard. In that instant the thing appeared closer, maybe ten feet away, the crimson glint of crusted blood visible around its wounds.

It whispered, *Jimmy.*

His blood turned to ice. He shot a glance at Eric nearing the road, strolling along innocently, unaware of the ghost, not seeing what Jimmy saw.

Unsettled but unafraid, Jimmy snarled, "What do you want? You leave me and my family alone."

The hum of an engine signaled an approaching car.

A reedy snicker came from the thing's ragged grin, and Jimmy blinked again. When he opened his eyes, it was gone.

"You ready?" Eric's voice came from right across the road.

Jimmy whirled around. The piercing screech of skidding tires stabbed his ears. Caleb Wilder stood dead-center in the road, arms outstretched in triumph. A speeding red SUV slammed on its brakes, jerked sideways, and careened into the other lane to miss him.

Eric turned toward the racket. The wall of ruby metal hurtled at him like the sledge of a giant hammer. Jimmy screamed from the top of his lungs, his warning lost in the squeal of rubber.

Eric raised his arms, bracing. The impact erased him in a flash. A solid boom and a heavy clunking beneath the vehicle—the sounds hit Jimmy like a slug to the gut. Halfway off the road, the SUV came to a standstill in a spray of mud and sod.

The driver's door slung open. A young woman hopped out, shaking her hands like trying to dry her nails.

Jimmy couldn't breathe.

The woman ran to the rear of the vehicle. Eric's body lay twisted, not moving. She leaned over him and gave a low, animal wail that churned Jimmy's stomach. She fell to her knees and pulled at her hair.

Another car pulled to a stop. Two people rushed out to help.

"It's not my fault!" the driver cried. "I saw another person! I had to swerve! He was in the middle of the road!"

The other couple covered their faces, shaking their heads.

"You!" the woman bawled, pointing at Jimmy. "You saw him, right? The man in the road? I swear, he was standing in the street!"

Eric's parents rushed from their home, shouting for their son, his mother's face withering as she drew near.

Jimmy stood there with his jaw open, speechless, and watched the world fall apart.

***

The next few days passed Jimmy in surreal slow-motion. He felt hollow inside.

At the viewing, Jimmy placed Eric's prized survival knife, cleaned and sheathed, alongside his body in the casket. Eric's parents had approved the gesture as a show of respect, agreeing their son would have wanted exactly that. Jimmy then mail-ordered an identical knife for himself—something to always keep as a reminder of their friendship.

After the burial, grief ate at Jimmy unlike anything he'd ever suffered. He'd never known a close friend to die, and the sorrow pulled him down like lead weights. He tried not to think of how Eric would never drive a car, or go to prom, hit a game-winning home run, or marry the love of his life. He tried not to dwell on those thoughts because they were vile and poisonous, and Jimmy already bore plenty of those.

His home life had sunk to an all-time low. The very atmosphere of the house had become so oppressive that joy seemed a distant memory. Nobody even spoke to each other. Caleb Wilder was killing his family from the inside-out.

At a loss for an answer, Jimmy picked up a few books and researched a number of famous hauntings, but had yet to find instructions on how to rid the house of an entity. The future looked bleak.

***

Saturday afternoon shrouded Trapper Valley in a gray blanket of cloud, but Jimmy walked to his mailbox with a rare air of high expectation. His package was due to arrive: a new hardened steel survival knife, complete with ball compass, hollow composite handle, fishing tools, wire saw, leather case plus an integrated pocket for a sharpening stone. The parcel had shown up, and Jimmy tore into it with a fervor he hadn't felt in days. He ripped open the plastic and marveled at the knife's beautiful black steel and pristine cutting edge. Eric had been right; it truly was a work of art.

Yet, standing there marveling at the knife made it impossible to ignore the awful memory of losing his friend. The trauma still raw, everything felt cold, too cold and too familiar. Jimmy looked around. The street deserted, the neighborhood seemed uncannily still and quiet, like a sailor describes the eye of a storm.

Jimmy once again felt that leering stare burn into him like the scope of a sniper, and his heart darkened. He turned to see Caleb Wilder standing across the street like a scarecrow.

The specter tilted its face, watching him from the very spot where Eric had met his end, and gave a wicked grin.

Pure hatred welled inside Jimmy. He clenched his teeth, and a fire stoked hot within him. He wanted nothing more than to stalk over to the thing and gash it to ribbons with his new razor-sharp weapon. But it would be useless to try, and Jimmy's powerlessness made him seethe.

From the corner of his eye, something caught his attention. To the rear of that wretched face, roughly thirty yards away, was Eric's rickety treehouse perched in a tall maple. The frayed rope ladder that dangled beneath hung completely still even though Jimmy could see perfectly well someone shimmying down to the ground.

Jimmy looked at the ghost of Caleb Wilder as it uttered with a tongueless hiss, *What are you afraid of, Jimmy?*

The thing did not notice what approached it from behind.

Jimmy's heart raced. His good friend Eric Hyde was marching across the lawn while pulling a large black knife from a leg-strapped leather sheath. He wore the same camo clothes as on the day of his death—and not a scratch on him. Eric's steely, square-jaw expression, like a soldier on a mission, gave Jimmy a sudden rush of confidence. He leveled a glare at Caleb, who gawked back through empty sockets.

"You're a grade-A scumbag, you know that?" Jimmy growled. Impossibly, his friend had already halved the distance between them. "You're one seriously sick puppy."

The thing only chuckled, a sound of tumbling dead leaves.

Eric drew within a few feet of reach.

"But you screwed up this time. You shouldn't have messed with my friend ..."

That's when Eric clamped his palm over Caleb Wilder's ruined face, lifting the bony figure from the ground with a single arm. In a spastic fit, the thing squirmed and writhed. Eric's eyes gleamed. He raised the knife high. With cobra speed, he thrust the blade into its right kidney area, eliciting a shocked but muffled moan.

... because Eric has been practicing.

Eric ripped out the knife then buried it hilt-deep into the thing's pale, skinny throat. With a flick of the wrist, he slashed it open from ear to ear.

Gagging and convulsing, the black figure crumpled to the ground hemorrhaging a thick, sooty dust from the gaping wounds. Its elbows folded and its face hit the grass. The thing shuddered and contorted. Then its skeletal frame bled away like spilled ink, disintegrating into the soil below. In a few seconds it was gone.

Jimmy leaned against the mailbox to steady himself. He took a deep breath of fresh air. It cooled his lungs, tasted crisp and clean.

Like breaking dawn, the day brightened. Clouds parted for a strong beam of sunlight that warmed his shoulders. A bird in the distance chirped a playful tune. Jimmy had the sense that the world around him was awakening from a long slumber.

Eric looked at him and said in a strangely distant voice, "Phase two." He sheathed his blade and smiled bigger than ever.

"Thanks, buddy," Jimmy said.

His friend lifted an arm and gave him a military-style salute. Then he turned and headed back to the treehouse, but vanished before making it to the rope ladder.

Wherever Eric was now, he seemed happy. And that meant a lot.

***

The music playing from inside his house surprised Jimmy as much as anything. He opened the door to the deep-bass baritone of Johnny Cash on the stereo, his dad's all-time favorite singer. In the kitchen he found his mother humming along while stacking sugar, eggs and chocolate chips on the countertop.

"I feel like making cookies," she greeted. "How does that sound?"

His father came around the corner carrying a paint pail and singing the chorus to "I Got Stripes." He kissed his wife on the cheek and gave Jimmy a wink. "I could use a hand if you're not too busy, son."

"Jimmy?" his mother said, snapping him out of a confused stupor. "That sound good to you?"

"I'm sorry. What'd you say?"

"Cookies... You want some?"

Jimmy looked around his home as though seeing it for the first time. The icy chill was gone, and Jimmy welcomed the sunny warmth that now filled the house. At long last, everything felt right again.

"Sure, Mom."

Cookies had never sounded better.

The End

Bloodbath in First Grade

On the opening day of school Laura Windham found a vase of water and pink roses on her desk. The headmaster had left the gift along with a note that read: *Good luck on your first day. Here's hoping things go smoothly and you don't get stuck with any bad apples. Happy teaching! – Principal Croker.*

Laura folded the note and placed it in a drawer, convinced there could be no such thing as a bad apple in a class full of young minds and fresh faces.

As the pupils filed in, she stood in front of her first-grade class with a broad smile to make everyone feel welcome. The students sat in six rows of desks. Some children stared at her, while others fidgeted or whispered to their schoolmates. One young girl with long black hair slumped in her chair at the back of the room and leered through her stringy bangs with a stark scowl.

"Hello, children," Laura greeted.

"Hello," replied a handful of kids.

"I'm Mrs. Windham." She walked to the blackboard, as apprehensive as the students about the new school and her first job as an educator. Molding young minds was a great responsibility. "It's pronounced like the words 'wind' and 'ham.'" She wrote them in chalk on the board, marking a hyphen between them. "Wind-ham ... *Windham.*"

A tow-haired girl with pink skin sat in a corner seat. "Hello, Mrs. Windham."

Laura bent down and favored her with a smile. "Hi there." She then stepped to her desk, picked up a notebook and addressed the class at large. "Welcome to Shady Brake Elementary. I'll be your first-grade teacher. I look forward to having fun with all of you as we learn lots of new things this year. Now I'm going to call roll. When I get to your name, please say 'here' and tell us something about yourself."

A murmur of soft responses shuffled through the classroom.

"Tommy Adams," she began.

A boy in the back seated next to the black-haired girl raised his hand. He had a headful of sandy curls and wore a white shirt with a purple smear on the collar. "Here!" he piped, "I'm Tommy and I like to go fishing. And I have a fish tank, too." He puckered his lips and wagged his hands beside his ears like fins. The class chuckled.

"Nice to meet you, Tommy," Mrs. Windham said. She scrolled down the list. "Myra Butler."

"That's me," said the tow-haired girl. "My name is Myra Butler, and I like unicorns and puzzles and baking cookies."

"Pleasure to make your acquaintance, Myra. Let's see … Jonathon Dunwoody."

A chubby kid with a buzz-cut shot up his hand and professed his love of Reese's Cups, Three Musketeers and Twix.

The black-haired girl's glower of disgust never softened as she eyeballed the other students. She wore a smudged black sweater and gray sweatpants with dry mud caked near the ankles. Laura made a mental note about the mud, then continued down the list with each child responding with their preferences for toys, food or recreational activities. As they did, the girl leveled each a withering gaze that bled utter contempt, as though every one of them had gravely wronged her in a most personal way. Such a shame, thought Laura. At such a young age she appeared to carry a weight far beyond her years, and Laura knew that some sort of heartache hid beneath all the anger. With kids that was always the case.

She called the last name on the list. "Vanessa Wilkins."

The unhappy girl locked eyes with her but did not answer. Instead, two brown pigtails jiggled on the far side of the classroom as a different girl said, "Here! I like cupcakes and riding bikes and swimming."

Something about the black-haired girl's bottomless eyes and her ominous stillness … she radiated a hatred more intense than anything Laura had ever seen from a child. Her soft features took a hard edge over the stiff angles of her grimace, like a strange flower on the verge of blossoming vast black petals that will darken everything around it.

"I'm sorry," Laura said to the girl, lifting her voice slightly to be heard in the back. "You don't seem to be on my list. What's your name?"

Without breaking her gaze, the girl slowly stood from her chair. Lifting a gray backpack from her lap, she pinched the zipper and slid it open. Her hand slipped into the pouch. She withdrew a wooden spool—no, not a spool, something longer. Skinny fingers gripped a handle, and on its end extended a thin, shiny rod. She had an icepick.

Laura's pulse quickened. "What on earth are—"

The girl leaned forward, and her eyes narrowed as thin as her lips. Her mouth opened with an earsplitting screech that cut through Laura's brain and chilled her bones. The students threw their hands to their ears.

With a mad snarl, the girl whipped around to Tommy Adams. Her arm curled in an uppercut that shoved the icepick beneath the boy's jaw. His head snapped back, and the tip shot out his mouth. She slammed his curly head onto his desk like Laura had seen her dad slap a fresh-caught crappie down to clean it.

The room exploded with screams. Tommy made a nasally mewling noise, struggling beneath the fishhook grip of the pick.

Laura screamed as well and shook her hands uselessly. She rushed between the rows and batted at the girl with open palms to ward her off. The girl ripped out the icepick and raised it high. It came at Laura with a gleaming point. She ducked. It snagged her sleeve and ripped the fabric. Laura stumbled backward.

Desks toppled as children tripped over each other in retreat. The girl lunged across a chair and stabbed a boy in the back. His head jerked back, his lips stretched tight. Eyes squinting, he fell over.

Most students ran to the opposite wall putting their teacher between them and the danger. Two boys leapt into a closet and held the door as a barricade. Others made a dash for the exit, but the mad girl loped across the furniture with animal speed and cut them off. With another screech she slashed the icepick and caught Jonathon Dunwoody in his chubby neck. His flesh opened like soft fruit, and a flood of dark blood poured over the floor as he collapsed and flopped around.

"Stop her, Mrs. Winston!" a child plead.

Laura snagged two kids by their collars and jerked them away from the girl, thrusting them behind her. She stood guard over the others without a plan and only a prayer. "For God's sake, someone get in here!" she screamed as loud as possible. Another teacher, a passing janitor—someone had to help.

Two ropes of unwashed hair draped down the girl's face as she hung her head low and leered up, eyes never straying from Laura. She stamped a foot forward, and the children gasped. The girl stalked ahead two more steps, and the kids shrieked. The icepick passed from one thin hand to the other, then back again eagerly, like she took pleasure in the pain it wrought.

Laura shrank back a couple of steps then realized she would soon run out of floor space. They all would. Windows covered half the wall behind them, but they tilted out at their tops and opened only six inches wide. Useless.

She grabbed the waste-basket beside her desk—a black cylinder of metal mesh—and held it as a shield. A cascade of papers fluttered down from it onto the linoleum floor.

The girl swung the icepick. Laura blocked it. The girl stabbed and jabbed, but Laura switched the basket back and forth to deflect her.

"Stop it, young lady! *Stop it!*"

Stabs came faster, harder, the icepick striking like an asp from the thrusting forearm.

"You drop that knife!" Laura screamed, baffled by the girl's strength and quickness.

But the girl dropped down and reached beneath her, slashing at Laura's legs, nicking her shin. Laura leapt up as the girl slipped forward in Jonathon Dunwoody's pooling blood. They both lost their balance, and Laura brought her weight down onto the basket, smashing down onto the young slasher. The girl smacked the floor face-first with a grunt. With a click and a whir, the icepick rolled away.

Bracing a knee atop the wastebasket with the girl struggling beneath, Laura took a deep breath then recognized the moment. She scrambled for the weapon. A boy stopped its roll beneath his sneaker. She reached down, grabbed the icepick and spun back around.

The girl pushed herself up and slowly wobbled to her feet. She tried to walk but staggered, visibly shaken.

Laura raised the blade over her shoulder. "Don't you *move!*"

The classroom door swung open. Mrs. Hetfield from across the hallway looked at all the carnage. Her hands went to her mouth. Her eyes expanded tenfold at the sight of Laura standing over the student while wielding the icepick. Then, like an apparition, she was gone again leaving only the funk of too much perfume.

"Get the police!" Laura cried after her. She turned back to the girl. "Listen, Miss. I don't know what's wrong with you, but this—what you're doing—it won't help. I'm here to help! I'm here to listen. We can work through this, but *please* stop hurting people. Let's talk through this."

Laura's breathing came in quick, wispy gasps. Her heart pattered against her breastbone.

"Stab her!" shouted a student from behind.

Fear of both death and failure tugged at Laura from two different sides and threatened to tear her in half, knowing that she literally held their means of escape in her sweaty palm—the sharpened steel cocked and ready—but that was an impossible choice to make: to kill a child, when her job was to help them.

The girl hissed and swatted the air between them, standing her ground. Her nose bled brightly down her lips.

"You can talk to me. You can trust me," Laura offered in as steady a voice as she could muster. "There's a problem at home, right? There's a problem that causes you to lash out like this? Because we can deal with those problems. You can trust me."

The girl growled, feral and inhuman. The poor child would require major psychiatric help to pull her from the darkness, and to talk her down from the frenzy seemed the best course of action. That she hadn't yet pounced after losing the weapon gave Laura a modicum of hope.

A rustle came from the hallway. Principal Croker rushed into the room wearing a coat and tie. The door banged against the stopper. His jaw dropped. "Not again!"

Mrs. Hetfield showed up in the hallway behind him, hopping around and tapping frantically on her phone.

"This little girl is sick," Laura told them.

The girl looked at them and gave a wildcat snarl.

"Stab her!" the principal ordered.

"What?" With the weapon still held high, Laura tightened her grip.

"I said stab her! While you have the chance! She's a killer, don't trust her. *Stab her!*"

Laura looked at the icepick, seven inches of metal death. Where the shaft met the hilt, the wood glistened with blood. Even if she decided to do it, to command her arm to send the steel point hurtling forward, Laura knew her muscles would lock up. Her body would revolt. Her elbow would freeze because she simply didn't have it in her, and Laura knew that fact with cold certainty.

"The girl is not what she looks like!" shouted Principal Croker.

Laura clenched her teeth, reared back … but hesitated.

The girl crouched down and sprang. The young body rammed into Laura, clutching her shoulders, spilling her backward. The weight heaved upon her chest made Laura trip over an upturned desk, and she smacked to the floor on her side. The girl snatched the icepick from her hand and crawled over, stomping Laura's cheek into her teeth.

The chorus of terrified voices rose to crescendo as the crowd of children burst from its cluster. Bawling, stumbling, falling, they all tried to flee. The girl moved like a threshing machine, spearing the blade through body and bone in a vicious fervor.

Myra Butler fell onto Laura fish-eyed, blank-faced and bleeding from her temple. Laura rolled her onto the floor. She stood up shakily as the crazed girl, bent over a body pinned to a desktop, stirred the hilt-deep blade around in Vanessa Wilkin's eye socket.

With every rotation of the handle in the girl's face, Laura's sanity swirled down a drain.

Principal Croker sprinted across the room to the vase of roses he'd left for Laura. He snatched the clear glass and ripped out the flowers. When he turned around an expression of fury lit his face like a halo of fire. He charged the girl, held up the vase and slung it around, gripping its base. Water flung from the opening in a fan of thick droplets that splattered the girl and the body of the Wilkins girl.

"Be gone creature! *And stay gone this time!*"

Where the liquid hit her, the girl's flesh sizzled and popped. Tendrils of smoke curled up from the wounds. Her blistering flesh billowed with smoke, and the howl that came from her lungs rattled the panes of the classroom windows. Her skin melted and dripped from the wounds like candle wax, spattering to the floor.

"Precious Jesus in heaven!" Mrs. Hetfield wailed from the doorway and covered her mouth.

Having fallen to her knees, the girl shuddered in a heap. The shirt and sweatpants peeled away from her rupturing body in ashen disintegration, revealing gray wet flesh beneath the human skin, webbed with veins and marbled a dull blue-gray like a bloated corpse. The girl, or whatever it was, quivered on its haunches. Then its ailing moans grew with strength and anger.

Principal Croker held a desk above his head. "Die. You abomination!" He hurled it, but the creature swatted it away with a screech. The thing's face now a featureless mass of folds and wrinkles, brown hair having molted away in dark clumps, it gave a raspy roar and rose back up. The girl was a girl no longer. The thing grunted and growled, then leapt to the ceiling and somersaulted as it did. It gripped the suspended grid between the acoustical tiles, using claws on feet and hands to hang inverted in a crawling position. The metal channels bowed beneath the weight.

"Oh, dear God!" Mrs. Hetfield cried.

Like some hellish crustacean it scuttled across the ceiling toward the hall where she stood. Mrs. Hetfield hit the floor, and it crawled through the top of the doorway out of sight.

"Damn!" Principal Croker chased it into the hallway, leap-frogging the teacher and tracking the ceiling as he pursued it.

At last, police sirens sounded their arrival somewhere outside.

Laura found herself resting in a ball on the bloody floor, knees tucked beneath her chin, arms hugging her shins, whimpering along with her surviving students.

Principal Croker soon came back through the door and barked some very angry words at her, but she had a difficult time following their meaning. They were lost in a tempest of shattered dreams, thundering with the ghastly snarls of child killers and the desperate screams of baby victims. Croker said something about following orders and learning lessons. Something about pragmatism versus idealism, and how whenever you have a killer cornered, you should always take them out. Then his temper seemed to wane. And he mentioned how this sort of thing hardly ever happens.

When a crowd gathered outside the door, the principal stopped talking. He looked at his hands. He looked at the dead children then turned away and gave a choking sob. His hands then went to his tie and straightened it. He sniffed once and swallowed.

"I'm sorry I said those things," he said to Laura in a much softer tone. He placed a hand on her shoulder. "It wasn't fair. I'm … I'm just a little overwhelmed right now. I thought this was all behind us. But you should get out of here. Get yourself cleaned up. You look very shaken. You're going to need to talk to someone. Get your head straight. This kind of trauma can haunt you." He glanced down the hallway. "I have to go speak to the police now."

As he stepped away, she managed to utter a few syllables. "W-w-wait. I don't understand."

Croker stopped at the doorway. "I know you don't. I'm sorry."

The world made no sense at that moment. None of what had happened should ever take place in a rational world, and Laura needed grounding in a rational world. She needed a touchstone for her sanity, and for Croker to give it to her.

"What happened here? What on earth happened *in my classroom?!*" The way those last three words sputtered out, Laura realized she was blubbering.

"I don't exactly have an explanation. Nothing that would make you feel better." He looked down the hall. "The police…"

"But you know something," Laura said. "There's something you're not telling me."

Principal Croker hung his head. He gave a long sigh and spoke at the ground. "You're right. I'm sorry. What can I say?" He looked up. "Welcome to Shady Brake."

Then he walked away.

The End

Hell Comes to the Burger Hut

A portly family of four sits at the front window of the Burger Hut, each of them stuffing their faces. The restaurant staff appears shorthanded—only three workers in sight, and they're all buried in their duties.

These hicks won't know what hit them.

My wife sits alone stationed at a corner table across the lobby, pretending to sip a fountain drink. She gives me a wink. Jet-black hair, deep blue eyes, and a smile to charm a snake. Natalie possesses a beauty that can leave a man speechless. I'm lucky to have her. She's the love of my life and my top operative.

We're stationed off I-65 in a suburban podunk called Trapper Valley, Alabama. I selected this place for its proximity to the freeway, but also because of its disgusting everyday Pax Americana.

Fast-food lovers are treated to cheap, wobbly plastic chairs scattered around eight rickety foldaway tables. Two condiment islands divide the lobby's black-and-white checkered floor from the long cashier's counter. Along the glass-paned front wall squats a row of three dining booths with a captain's view of the interstate on-ramp.

At the table next to us, a skinny boy with an overbite takes a seat across from a chubby girl with acne. The teenagers hold hands and close their eyes. They bow their heads and mumble something.

Amen, he says.

The kid removes a small carton from a greasy paper sack, places it in front of him and opens the top. The smell of cooked meat clouds the air. He plunges a fork into his chili dog. Visions of slaughterhouses and offal piles rush through my mind. I hear the squealing of pigs and the baying of dying cattle. I see the glassy, terror-filled eyes of the animals, and see their gaping, pleading mouths calling for help that will never come.

The boy lifts up a plug of the frank as a brown lump of spiced beef plops off the fork. He shoves the bite onto his tongue and chews with his mouth open, smacking his food as juice runs down his chin.

A gray-haired man in a leather jacket walks through the Burger Hut's front door. He greets the woman at the register, "Afternoon, Mabel."

"Howdy, Mayor!" Mabel pushes her bifocals back on her nose and flashes the man a grin.

This is a huge stroke of luck. With a politician in the fold, we can count on a wall-to-wall news blitz. They call that kind of publicity "earned media," and it has more reach than any paid advertisement.

The only other people present are two old biddies having coffee and a loner with a scruffy beard and hunting jacket. He's the type to carry a pistol under that jacket, so I watch him like a hawk.

The time is prime, because the mayor and Mabel are distracted in conversation, and I can tell by Natalie's expression we're on the same page: start with the big fish; don't let him get away.

From her seat, she gives me a glance, one eyebrow raised.

I respond with a nod.

Ready. Steady. Go.

Natalie slips her dark sunglasses on. She rises onto those long, shapely legs and strides across the room in a black mini-skirt and stiletto heels. I noticed Scruffy Hunter eyeballing her earlier, but now when she passes, he looks up from his burger and really drinks her in. It's clear on his face that he knows she "ain't from around here."

I unzip the duffle bag in the chair to my left.

Since the mayor has his back turned, Mabel is the first to notice Natalie. She shifts her eyes from my wife to the mayor and back, unsure how to proceed with the six-foot siren slinking up beside him on the opposite side of the cash register.

Natalie draws up about twelve inches from the mayor, clicks her heels together, and looks at him like he was the Christmas gift she'd always wanted.

When he turns, he actually flinches at the sight of her beauty, his head pulling back, chin tucked in, then he breaks into one of those "vote for me" smiles.

"Why, hellooooo!" he gushes, extending his hand to her. It's obvious from the corny honk of his voice that this guy is a natural panderer. One who loves the ladies.

"Hiiii," she replies in a hiss, short but silken. She should be an actress. "I hear you're the mayor."

She glances back to her corner then adjusts her stance. She wants a more flattering angle for the video camera live-streaming from the tiny tripod where she'd been sitting. Nobody ever got famous for the back of their head.

"That's me." The mayor chuckles. "Guilty as charged." His eyes crawl over Natalie's body, and he can't seem to quit his goofy grin. He looks younger than his gray hair would suggest, and the way he's practically feeding from Natalie's palm tells me he's accustomed to using his position to drop as many panties as he can get away with.

Mabel reappears from nowhere. She slides a paper sack across the counter and tugs on his jacket sleeve. "Your Whammy burger's ready, Mayor."

"Thank you, Mabel." He reaches across his chest and snatches the bag with his left hand without ever dropping his right, which is still awaiting Natalie's handshake. He never takes his eyes off my wife.

The mayor tells her, "I don't believe we've met before."

Natalie touches the red plastic straw of her jumbo fountain drink to the corner of her lips. She stares at him through two black lenses and says, "No, I don't believe we have."

When she takes the mayor's hand, I can tell he's under her spell. I stand up and hook the duffle bag over my shoulder.

"My name is Jimmy Grayson, mayor of Trapper Valley. And I'm sure I haven't seen *you* around town. I've got a knack for faces, and I know I'd remember yours."

"You're right, mayor," she says. "You'd remember me. Because once somebody meets me, they're never the same again."

Natalie releases his hand, peels the lid off her drink, and lays the lid with the straw on the countertop to her left. "My name is The Red Queen, and I'm with the National Humanitarian Front."

He tilts his head and squints but doesn't seem to process what she said. His grin returns. "Well, on behalf of our fine city, I'd like to formally welcome you, and offer one of our famous local delicacies—a Whammy burger! With the works!"

When he extends the paper sack to her, Natalie glares at it with contempt. The mayor has unknowingly flipped a switch, and I can already feel the heat rising in the room.

"I. Don't. Eat. Meat." Each of her words, a drop of acid.

The mayor's smile fades.

Natalie hurls her drink. The liquid inside splashes him right in the face. Mabel gasps while Natalie jumps back to dodge the splatter.

The mayor's head and jacket are soaked, and a new chemical odor joins the smell of sizzling fat. He drops the burger sack and holds his arms out to his sides, looking himself over in disbelief and retreating backward in little steps. He's too distracted to notice me approaching him.

"Why did you..." he began. "What did you pour on me?"

Natalie throws back her head and laughs, cold as ice. "What did I pour on you?" she says. "Why, it's our secret sauce! So, it's a secret…"

She pulls a long-stem barbecue lighter from her rear pocket, and the mayor's angle doesn't let him see the yellow flame click to life behind her back.

God, I love her.

I lift my sawed-off from the duffle bag.

When Ms. Mabel sees me, she tries to warn him. "Mayor, behind you!"

This is helpful, because the mayor turns around to me with his dripping, bewildered face—and away from Natalie, who touches the lighter to his collar.

In a bright flash, he bursts into flames. His scream is worthy of a horror-movie heroine. Everyone in the lobby panics. Everyone except me and Natalie.

I spin on the Scruffy Hunter, who is reaching into his jacket. Is he armed? Having a heart attack? Doesn't matter. I pull the trigger to the sound of thunder. The buckshot blasts him off his chair.

The restaurant workers rush up from the back. Natalie draws the nine from her purse and opens fire. She hits one of them in the chest, and he collapses against a wall. Mabel flees out of sight toward the rear of the building.

The mayor is writhing on the floor and choking on smoke. His clothes turn black like burnt paper. He tries to bat the flames off his face, but his skin sticks to his hands and peels away.

Natalie leaps over the service counter to chase down the workers in the kitchen. I hear the gunshots and know she's got things covered.

The two teens are dashing for the front. I rack the shotgun and fire. A spray pattern rips across the boy's back as he spills out the double doors onto the sidewalk. The girl ahead of him turns back and shouts "Danny!" but at the sight of me and my gun barrel, she keeps running.

A lot of banging and clamor from the kitchen, then I hear a shriek that makes me freeze. Someone stumbles out of the kitchen to the front counter, moaning and slapping the walls blindly. I recognize those flesh-embedded bifocals. It's Mabel, only now she's practically unrecognizable, her face blistered and contorted. My wife emerges behind her with a grin, and I realize she must have somehow shoved Mabel down into a fry vat, boiling her in oil.

"Oh, shut up," Natalie says to her. She steps over to Mabel, puts her gun to the woman's temple, and *pow!*

The two elderly women are shuffling toward a side entrance. Natalie vaults back over the countertop on a single hand, takes aim and fills their backs with bullets. They fall together in a heap on the floor.

This only leaves the family of fat people frozen in the middle booth.

I step up to their table. The mother is gripping the edge of the table in the throes of some sort of fit. She's hyperventilating, rocking back and forth with her head thrusting to and fro.

The father, in his yellow Hawaiian-print shirt, has his arm around one of his chunky sons. The kid is crying into his dad's chest. The man's other hand is a trembling fist on the table. His face is pasty white, his eyes splayed and watery.

"This is your fault. You realize that, right?" I switch my gaze between each of the parents and tap their trays of half-eaten burgers with the shotgun. "This is what you call food? This is what you teach your children? This is not *food*."

"Please don't hurt us," the father says. "These are my sons Bryan and Keith—"

"Shut up," I tell him. Anything he might say is meaningless. Projecting my voice for the recorded audio, I ask, "What if this meat had been ground from the flesh your sons? Would you call it *food* then? This isn't *food*, it's *violence*. And violence begets violence. We are proof of that."

I rack the gun again. The father tries to stand. He opens his mouth to protest. I shove the barrel between his teeth and squeeze the trigger. The back of his head explodes, painting the window behind him.

I expect more screaming, but they are too shocked to speak. The kid who has bits of his dad speckling his cheek makes a mewling noise and shrinks into the corner.

"Stand up," I order the woman.

"No, no, please no," she whimpers.

Natalie walks up to my side. "Stand the fuck up!"

The woman turns beet-red and mumbles gibberish. She looks like she might liquefy and ooze onto the floor, then Natalie presses a switchblade against her pudgy neck, and the mom goes rigid and shuts the hell up.

"Stand," Natalie tells her.

The mom struggles to her feet.

"Walk."

She slouches ahead as instructed—a drab-looking woman with dishwater hair.

Halfway across the lobby, Natalie orders, "On your knees."

The mom closes her eyes and obeys. They're both facing Natalie's camera.

Standing behind the woman, my wife looks into the lens. "We're from the National Humanitarian Front and we're here to make a statement! For ages, you people have killed the innocent to satiate your gluttonous appetites. Those of us with a sense of empathy have tried to reason with you and persuade you to change your ways. Still, you persist, and we now have no recourse but to take an eye for an eye."

I step next to Natalie, right into what should be the video frame, just like we practiced. I glare straight ahead, rack the shotgun, and shout, "Viva la revolution!"

Then, I aim. The blast spreads the mother's face all over the live-streaming camera lens. This theatrical touch was Natalie's idea, and while I haven't seen it from our viewers' perspective, I bet it looked gnarly.

"This is the new reality," Natalie declares. "Today is a day of change! Those of us who value peace, nature, and equality can no longer sit idly by as the flesh-eaters continue their barbaric exploitation of animals. The time of enlightenment is at hand. We are the N.H.F., and to punish the guilty is the most humane thing we can do in our new society."

I rack the gun and blow the camera to pieces, ending our live feed. This "explosive finale" was another of my wife's ideas.

I turn to Bryan and Keith. The young boys are now little more than shellshocked mounds of jelly. I give Natalie a shrug, then walk toward the car. Time to split.

As I reach the door, I turn around and half-expect to see Natalie stabbing the boys with her knife. Instead, she's jogging to catch up with me, sporting a coy expression as if she knows what I'd been thinking. And she probably does.

She loops her arm around mine, and we push through the double doors together, heading to our car.

Just outside, the crack of gunfire. The door behind us shatters.

"Go!" I shout to Natalie. I rack my last shell, but I've got no idea who's shooting at us or from where. Based on the spray of glass, the shooter is probably to our right. We haul ass to the left. Lucky for us, that's where we'd parked.

Someone fires twice more, but we make it across the parking lot. Natalie is ahead of me. I slide in loose gravel and fall on my hip. More shots ring out.

Natalie spills forward.

NO!

I scramble to my feet and run to her side. I see blood. *Blood!* I scoop her up. She's not responding. Throwing her arm over my neck, I hoist her by the ribs, spinning around to see the mystery shooter take aim at us from the far side of a Taurus. It's the chubby girl with acne, Danny's girlfriend, armed with a pistol. I thrust out the twelve-gauge and fire a one-handed shot that only blasts the paint off the top of the Ford. But the girl ducks for cover, and that's what I need. I break for it, dragging Natalie with me. We get to the Jeep, and I stuff her into the passenger seat then roll across the hood to the driver's side.

I leap into the vehicle. The keys are waiting. I crank the ignition. Another gunshot, and glass sprinkles onto my lap. I duck down in the seat, throw the gear into reverse and peg the gas. The jeep lurches backward. We bang into another car. I cut the wheel and jam it into drive, peeking out the window to see the teenager realigning her sights. With a stomp on the accelerator, we swerve out of the parking lot, screeching the tires, and bound onto the road headed for the freeway on-ramp.

I hear one more shot, but it goes astray, and now we're speeding hell-for-leather away from the scene of the crime. Natalie is leaning against the car door.

"Sweety? Honey? Can you hear me? You okay?"

She makes a noise. I can't tell what she says, but it's a *noise* dammit! That's *something*!

"Look at me, honey. How bad are you hurt?"

She groans and sighs. She twists toward me and touches her forehead. Her right eye is a red ruin.

"Oh, baby, I'm so sorry."

"My head hurts..." she mutters and leans back against the door, closing her one good eye.

I merge onto the interstate and hit power on the radio. I dig through static and top-40s channels until I hit a news broadcast.

"*...The shooting in Dallas is the fifth attack reported today across the United States, with similar incidents taking place near Pittsburg, Detroit, Los Angeles and Memphis. Speculation is mounting that these separate events are coordinated attacks tied to domestic terrorism.*"

It's really happening.

I scan for a different channel and hear a local anchor say:

"*...Breaking news—we're getting an advance report of some sort of mass casualty event at a fast-food restaurant off I-65 near exit 272. That's the Trapper Valley exit. Brenda, what's the latest word on this?*"

Just wait until our video goes viral. It's going to be a hit.

"Mission accomplished, baby!" I tell Natalie. "We are now part of something much bigger than ourselves. They'll be talking about this day for the rest of our lives."

We're zipping down the freeway in pace with traffic, and nobody around seems to have any idea that we're two mass murderers making our escape. Two revolutionaries.

"You gonna be okay, hon?" I ask.

Natalie barely grunts a response, but I know she's exhausted. I should let her rest. A shame about her eye, but we'll get her all fixed up. And one thing's for sure, my wife will look smokin' hot in an eyepatch.

I pop open the center console. I pull out a beef stick and snap into a Slim Jim, picturing a cattle gun pressed to the head of a cow. With a sharp pop, a bolt penetrates the skull. The animal shudders and falls. The meat is so salty, spicy and damned tasty.

Truth is, we don't give a shit about anyone else's cause or agenda. Natalie and I are in it for the glory, and there's a whole lot of people all over the world who will celebrate everything we just did.

The End

Let 'em Have It

Jaylen Reynolds recognized the new kid in class at Trapper Valley High. They had gone to the same elementary school four counties away. He had a face Jaylen would never forget, nor would anyone else who'd been in Mrs. Harper's homeroom that terrible day back in fifth grade.

Now the boy sat two rows over, head down, scanning the classroom suspiciously like any teen who found themselves plunked into a new and unfamiliar high school. Surrounded by strangers, he looked lost and maybe lonely, like he could use a friend. Jaylen decided to be that friend, and finally nail down some answers to the biggest mystery of his childhood.

A bell screamed overhead.

As everyone filed out of the room into the hallway. Jaylen asked him from behind, "You went to Dusky Cove Elementary, didn't you?"

The boy stopped in his tracks. His posture tensed up. Slowly he glanced over his shoulder. "Talking to me?"

"Yeah." Jaylen shifted around to face him.

The guy no longer wore eyeglasses like when he was younger. He had curly black hair and had grown a foot taller than Jaylen, but Jaylen knew it was him all the same.

"I went there, too. I recognize you. How you doing?" Jaylen introduced himself, stuck out a hand, and flashed a big smile.

The boy had lanky arms and legs, and sprigs of his messy hair poked out from behind his ears. With wary green eyes, he looked Jaylen up and down, but after a moment accepted the handshake.

"I'm Trip."

Jaylen had finally located Trenton Hoyt Peterson III, or "Trip" as his parents had nicknamed him. He'd learned the kid's identity from all the old gossip, but didn't want to say so and give off a creepy stalker vibe just seconds after they'd become reacquainted.

"Nice to meet you, Trip. You just move here?" Jaylen asked as another class full of students emptied into the hallway and flowed around them. "Come on, I'll walk with you."

They both turned and headed toward the locker bay.

"Two weeks ago." Trip spoke in a soft voice as if abiding by some sort of noise ordinance, despite the rabble in the crowded corridor.

"Me and Mom moved here two years ago for her job," Jaylen said. "It's a nice enough place, I guess, if you like white people."

Trip glanced at him sideways.

"Don't worry," Jaylen said with a wink. "I'm okay with white people."

Trip's mouth twitched at the corner.

"These folks need me around here," Jaylen continued, "'cause ain't nobody else got rhythm." He broke into a dance step.

At that, Trip gave a small chuckle.

"For real, though. It's kinda hard not to feel a little different in this vast sea of whiteness."

"Is that right?"

"Sometimes, you know, I feel sorta like an outsider. Probably like you're feeling right now, being new here and all."

"I guess so." Trip shrugged and stopped walking. "My locker's down here." He tilted his head at a bay of metal cabinets. Other kids milled around it like bees in a hive.

"Cool," Jaylen said. "Mine's up the hallway."

"Okay, then. I'll see you around."

Jaylen nodded. "All right. See you."

They had much more to talk about.

***

The only class Jaylen shared with Trip was biology, but he was happy to see him seated alone during lunch the next day at the end of a table.

"How's it going, Trip? Mind if I take a seat?"

Trip gave a nod, and Jaylen took the seat across from him. Both their meal trays had a half apple, a small carton of chocolate milk and a square slice of pizza with nearly identical puddles of grease pooling in their centers. Trip sipped his milk. Jaylen bit his apple.

"You could fill a lamp with all the oil that seeps out of one slice of school pizza," Jaylen said with his mouth full.

Trip looked at his plate like it were a dead possum. "No way I'm putting that in my mouth."

The cafeteria, wide and long with exits at both ends, had a buffet counter along one wall where students selected their food and then joined their peers somewhere among the stratified class system that comprised the high school lunchroom.

In a town the size of Trapper Valley, everyone knew everyone else, at least by face if not name, but with school in session everyone was assigned labels and social cliques. The place had its wealthy elites, its athletes, its computer nerds and its future convicts, and the birds of a feather all ate lunch together.

Jaylen didn't buy into the system. He didn't fit in and told himself he didn't want to.

"Who do you usually eat with?" Trip asked him.

"I like the view near the cheerleaders," Jaylen said. "But they don't talk to me much. Most of the other black guys are on the basketball or football team. They're okay, but I didn't make the teams on account of me being so short, so they don't really see me on the same level. Those square-looking dudes over at the next table spend all their time playing some game where they pretend like they're wizards or dragons. And those three dudes behind them, wearing army jackets, think they're in some sort of survival militia preparing for World War III. Not really my thing. So, I don't have a usual place to sit. I kind of float around."

Trip looked across the lunchroom at all the jabbering kids. "Seems like every other high school," Trip said. "They all suck."

"Where'd you go after Dusky Cove? I mean, before you came here. You left way before I did."

Trip slurped his milk and peered up with an eyebrow raised. "You remember when I left? Sounds like you remember a lot about me."

Jaylen took a deep breath, held it, then released a long sigh. "Okay, man. I'm going to level with you. I remember everything. I was there in Mrs. Harper's class that day. I was sitting in the back. No way I could ever forget what happened, and I know there ain't no way you could, either."

The color drained from Trip's face. He became fidgety, popping his knuckles. "Shit."

"Look, man, don't freak out," Jaylen said. "I don't plan on saying anything to anyone. This is between you and me.

But you gotta understand that what happened back then is going to haunt me for the rest of my life."

Trip cut him a sharp look. "Yeah? Well, me too. That's why I keep trying to put it behind me!"

"I know. I understand. But I got questions. Burning questions. And you're the only person who might can answer them."

"I don't want to talk about it."

"Why? What are you afraid of?"

Trip met his eyes again, this time with a hard, unflinching stare. He leaned across the table and said with more hiss than a whisper, "What am I *afraid* of? Don't you understand? Didn't you hear all the rumors? Weren't you *there?* Those rumors were true. It was all *my fault!* I caused it. And I'm afraid of ever causing it to happen again."

The fear in his eyes looked genuine, and Jaylen was relieved it wasn't fury. He thought for a moment, and when Trip grabbed his tray to leave, Jaylen put a hand on it.

"Trip," he said in a voice as calm and comforting as he could muster. "Please don't go. I'm a friend. And you just told me two important pieces of information—two things that convinced me I'm going to stay your friend. If you'll let me."

"What are you talking about?"

Jaylen waved a hand for him to sit back down. Trip, who was hovering in a crouch, slowly lowered himself back into the seat.

"You admitted that you caused it. And that's what I always suspected," Jaylen said. "But you also said you didn't mean to, and that's also what I always suspected."

Jaylen dropped his head. "I swear I didn't mean to."

"I believe you, Trip. I really do."

After all, figured Jaylen, how could any 10-year-old kid have ever intended to cause such a horrible turn of events?

***

Mrs. Harper's fifth-grade class had been studying creative writing. Each student wrote a short story, and every day during that particular school week, four of the children got to read theirs aloud in class.

Jaylen had already read his story on Monday, about a fireman who tried to rescue a cat from a tree, only for the cat to fly away as soon as he reached it because it was a rare breed of flying feline.

It was now Friday, and the day's stories had thus far entailed a little girl winning a cupcake-baking competition that gained her international glory and acclaim. One kid told of digging a hole in his back yard that led to Mars, which he colonized with his friends, conquered the Martian race, and then returned to earth with an army of enslaved aliens to exact revenge on his older brother.

Jaylen sat in the very back of the room, doodling his own space alien on the title page of his English textbook, when a young, spectacled Trip Peterson approached the front of the class holding a spiral-wired notepad. He was short and thin with straight curly black hair and a white collared shirt that hung half untucked like ice cream dripping from a cone. Jaylen didn't know him much, as the kid kept mostly to himself. But Jaylen enjoyed listening to the other students' stories, so he laid down his pencil and paid close attention.

Mrs. Harper, a plump woman with wavy hair and a pleasant smile, sat at her desk with her hands folded together. She gave Trip a nod that he could begin.

Trip cleared his throat and lifted the notebook to chin level. "This story is called 'The Crazy Thing that Happened One Day in Fifth Grade.'"

Jaylen, struck by the title, angled his ear to hear the details. After all, *he* was in fifth grade, too, and this story could just as well be about *him*.

"My teacher gave everyone an assignment to write a short story," Trip read. "They could write about anything they wanted. The students were supposed to use their imagination and be very creative. One of the students wanted to impress all his schoolmates with the most exciting story he could possibly come up with. He thought and thought, and started many stories but then threw them away because he thought they were dumb ideas. Finally, he came up with a master plan. The idea was so amazing that it would most definitely blow all his friends' minds."

This was getting good, and Jaylen leaned eagerly over his desk to learn how it would turn out.

"One night after his parents had gone to bed, the boy stayed up late to write his amazing story. Then, after all his hard work, came the day he finally got to read it in class. But when he told the story, something terrible happened. He didn't realize, but it was a magic story that could drive people insane when they heard it."

Gripped by the plot twist, Jaylen clenched his fists in suspense.

"And that's exactly what happened to his teacher," Trip said. "She went mad when she heard it. She started killing all the boy's classmates—"

With a wet smack, a splatter of red darkened Trip's white shirt. He stopped reading. Jaylen saw two dark droplets gleam on the lenses of the boy's eyeglasses. Time froze in a strange moment of silence, and then shattered with a shrill scream.

A chorus of screams erupted from all around, and Jaylen saw Mrs. Harper standing two desks away with a long, wooden handle clutched in her grip. She jammed a heeled foot into the chest of a seated student and jerked the blade of an axe out of the kid's split skull. Eyes crazed, her tongue licking the corners of her mouth, she lifted the axe high overhead.

Desks toppled. Kids dashed out the exit—others were petrified. The teacher hacked the blade into the neck of a squealing little blonde girl, who always sat in the front row.

Someone threw a book at her, but that didn't slow Mrs. Harper. She gave a monstrous howl, whirled around, and caught a fleeing boy in the back with the axe.

A rush of fifth-graders trampled past Trip, jostling him to the floor. His glasses skittered across the linoleum.

Jaylen snapped from his stupor when Mrs. Harper set sights on him and began kicking the desks out of the way as she plowed in his direction. He darted through an open aisle and speared through the doorway. Trip ran alongside him, his face ghostly pale.

The balding principal, Mr. Brown, sprinted down the hallway toward the classroom with his necktie tapering over his shoulder.

"No!" Jaylen warned as he flew past. "Don't go in there!"

The principal paid no attention. He neared the class as Mrs. Harper burst through the door, baring teeth in a wicked sneer.

"What on earth is going on?!" Mr. Brown shouted.

With a swing from her hip, she plunged the axe into his chest. For a moment Mr. Brown hung there, twitching on the end of the wooden handle like a prize bug on a pin. Then his knees buckled, and he collapsed. Mrs. Harper shook him off the blade.

The shrieks of more teachers pierced Jaylen's eardrums, and he turned to find the halls filling with terrified administrators. Jaylen had seen enough. He'd seen too much.

A flood of terror tightened the muscles of his face. Tears gushed out, and he ran through the hall, through the crowd, heading for fresh air and to put a safe distance between himself and the madness. He slowed only once to glance at the weeping face of Trip Peterson, who trembled against a wall in the wake of his magic story. Jaylen banged through the school's double doors and spilled into the courtyard. Other crying kids followed his lead.

Police sirens sang from around the corner. Every cop in town must have taken the call, and a squadron of black-and-white cruisers descended on the school.

Oh, thank you, Jesus, thought Jaylen, as the officers rushed into the building with their hands on their holsters.

Thank the Lord for the cops.

II

Back at Trapper Valley, Jaylen convinced Trip to accompany him for a walk after school to pick up some new comics at Burnside Books—and to pick his brain about magical stories. The two walked side by side, backpacks slung over their shoulders, as Jaylen kicked a rock along the way.

"Has anything that crazy ever happened since Dusky Cove?"

"I don't write stories anymore," Trip said.

A chill breeze blew dead leaves down the sidewalk in a swirl of reds and browns.

Jaylen glanced at his new friend, who strolled with his head down, tracking the ground. "That's not what I asked."

Trip gave a sigh, which meant he didn't want to answer the question, but Jaylen had learned that persistence could pay off. "Something else *did* happen!" he shouted. "Holy cow! What? You've gotta tell me!"

A trio of girls walking ahead, all skirts and hair barrettes, turned and made disapproving faces at them and raised their noses.

"Shhhh!" Trip snapped at him.

"Sorry," Jaylen said in a lowered voice. "I don't mean to geek out, but *Trip!* I mean ... if you made it happen *again,* then it must mean, like, you've got some sort of *super power!*"

"Power?" Trip shook his head. "It's not a power. It's a *curse!* Whenever I write stories, people get hurt. I don't want to *hurt* people."

Jaylen's imagination swirled with possibilities. Could Trip bring back the dinosaurs? Could he write a cure for cancer? Could Trip write them both the power of flight or invisibility or just a zillion dollars in cash?

"If you're serious ... I mean, *whoa!*" Jaylen said. "If you can really make things happen just by writing about them, you could practically rule the *world!*"

Trip sighed again. "You don't get it. When I write about stuff, yeah, the things do somehow come true. But I can't control it. I never know what's going to happen. I mean, where do you think Mrs. Harper got her axe that day? She got it from me. From my *mind.* I guess it just materialized from my story. How could I have known that would happen? I never would have written it. All those kids—dead. And the principal, Mr. Brown—*dead.* See, I didn't write about that stuff specifically. I didn't want them to be murdered. But it happened just the same, all because of a stupid story I made up ... that I somehow set into motion."

Trip stopped walking and rubbed his temples. The subject had obviously burdened him for a long time. "What I mean is, sure, I wrote that Mrs. Harper became a maniac, but she took it from there," he continued. "That's the problem. I can start a story, but I never know exactly how it will end."

Jaylen processed this information. "You said something else happened after Dusky Cove. You wrote another story, right? What went wrong?"

Trip gave him a troubled look then his gaze drifted away. He told Jaylen about the school bus. "It wasn't as gruesome as fifth grade. But still ..."

***

After Dusky Cove, Trip's family moved to podunk little Shady Brake, the next town over from Trapper Valley. His weekday routine required him to catch the Shady Brake Middle School bus each morning and afternoon. Being the new kid on the block, he hadn't yet made any friends and spent the commute sitting alone, reading a book or sketching monsters in a notepad.

It didn't take long for an oversized seventh-grader named Chase Battle to notice Trip's sketches and take umbrage with their artistic merit.

"Look at these stupid cartoons," Chase would shout as he ripped a handful of papers from the notepad he'd snatched from Trip's hands. He would slide into the aisle of the bus with the sketches held high above his head and out of Trip's reach, leafing through the stack, mocking each one as "lame," "dumb," or "doesn't look right at all" before dropping them to the grimy bus floor and stamping them underfoot.

This became a near-daily routine. Chase taught Trip that drawing on the bus was strictly prohibited, and after a while Trip duly abided by the rules. The written word, however, did not seem to offend Chase, which Trip attributed to the boy's suspected lack of literacy.

The time had come for Trip to write another story. And he wrote it on the bus after school about an ogre-like bully who had no appreciation for the arts. He wrote it about a big kid who singled out a smaller kid, one who drew cartoon monsters. The bully targeted this kid for Indian burns and ear-thumps and snot rockets every afternoon on the ride home. But, according to Trip's story, the bully finally exhausted the kid's patience. And, unbeknownst to the bully, the kid that he targeted was secretly the mastermind of a school-wide network of student vigilantes whose mission was to band together and confront injustice at every turn, and stop it in its tracks.

On this particular afternoon, Trip wrote the words THE END on his notepad after completing the story and turned to a new page. On that fresh paper lined with light blue ink, he drew a fanged hairy beast with one claw raised in a middle-finger salute.

Chase noticed this.

"Well, well, well. Looks like the fartsy-artist is back at his queer little drawings," Chase said over Trip's shoulder as he sketched the finishing touches on the monster. "I thought we decided we were gonna stop this silly crap, Peterson. You're breaking the rules."

Chase snatched the paper from the pad and raised it for inspection. "You trying to be a wise-ass, Peterson? Who is this guy supposed to be shooting a bird at?"

Trip stood up, turning to the rear of the bus to face Chase. The other students sat silent, stone-faced, their eyes ticking from Trip to Chase and back to Trip.

"Is he supposed to be flipping off *me*, you little twerp?"

Trip looked over the crowd of his peers, at their clenched teeth and their balled fists. Some held heavy books, others wielded sharpened pencils. And they awaited their orders.

He looked his rival dead in the eye and said, "Yeah, Chase. It's you that I'm telling to kiss off." Trip snapped his fingers.

The other kids took the cue.

They swarmed Chase in a wave of scrawny bodies, diving over the seats and pouncing onto his shoulders. They latched onto his neck and head, overtaking him like hungry piranha, snarling and growling, clawing and biting.

Chase swung and elbowed in a fury. He'd knock away one kid, but three more would take their place, attacking from all sides.

Trip felt a smile creep across his face. A surge of adrenaline buzzed through him. *The story worked! Pick on me, will ya?!*

Chase screamed like a Hollywood actress, all high-pitched and spiraling with sheer mortal terror. The school bus jerked to a halt, and Trip steadied himself on a seatback to keep from falling into the aisle.

"What the heck's going on back there!" shouted the lady bus driver, her plump face red with anger.

Bawling and fighting, Chase kept disappearing in a hail of fists and kicking feet. He sank between two seats, begging for help beneath a dogpile of kids who ripped and tore at him with rabid energy. Trip saw Chase's arm reach up and bat blindly at the air. The arm was bleeding.

"Stop it!" Trip commanded. "He's had enough!" He shoved forward and pulled two kids off Chase, then a third, each of them acquiescing as soon as they realized Trip was calling off the onslaught. Gradually the crowd simmered down and relented, returning to their seats and leaving the bully shivering in a ball on the floor.

Trip stood over Chase, whose nose bled, his face swollen. Teeth marks pocked his skin. Chase trembled and looked up.

"Never bother me again," Trip told him. "Or anyone else on this bus."

And from that day forward, Chase Battle duly abided by the new rules.

***

"Those kids would've killed him," Trip told Jaylen. "You should have seen it. They were crazed—*possessed*—or something. If I hadn't stepped in, Chase Battle would be nothing but a grease spot in the back of the bus."

From the sound of the guy, Jaylen wondered if that would have been such a terrible outcome. "Did anybody know you caused it to happen?"

Trip shook his head. "Just me. The other kids didn't seem to remember anything. Chase's mom tried to make a Federal case out of it, raising all sorts of hell with the school principal, but none of the students claimed to have seen the fight. At first, I thought it was all just a scheme to stay out of hot water; everyone on the bus was involved, but nobody wanted to fess up and get in trouble. The thing is, I think they were telling the truth. None of them had any recollection of what happened."

For Jaylen, every new piece of information inspired new and vital questions. Could Trip really control peoples' minds and then erase them of the memory? Jaylen wouldn't have believed a word if he hadn't already seen such craziness first-hand.

"Ever tried to help anyone with a story?" Jaylen asked.

"Once. Tried to help a dog. He'd been hit by a car in front of our house. I figured it was worth a shot. I wrote one little sentence and then 'The End'."

"And?"

"And I'd written: 'The dog stops hurting.'" Trip shrugged. "He died immediately."

Jaylen stared at his shoes then looked up. "That could have been natural causes."

Trip found his own rock and gave it a kick down the street. "I guess it could've been."

"Man," Jaylen said with a shake of the head. "I've gotta tell you, this whole thing is the strangest story I've ever heard."

"Strangest I've ever heard, too."

"I've never been good at writing," Jaylen said. "I'm more of a reader. My stories always sucked."

"That's not true. You've just got to practice. The flying cat—that was pretty cool."

Jaylen looked up and chuckled. "You remembered!"

Trip smiled. "It was awesome! How could I forget?"

They strolled into the Burnside Books parking lot with Jaylen still shaking his head. "Man, I wish I could write."

"Yeah," Trip said. "Me, too."

III

Dissecting a cat is a team-building exercise. This was the firm belief of the balding and bifocaled biology teacher, Mr. Kirby, who administered his anatomy lesson by dividing the class into groups of four, each team to share a cat. The big event was scheduled for the end of the week. However, before the students would be allowed to sink their first scalpel, they would have to complete a written test identifying the different organs and their corresponding function in the body. The group would be judged as a whole, prompting lunchtime study sessions to divide the workload—or to determine that at least *someone* on the team could answer the questions correctly.

"Spleen!" said Becky Morgan with a bright grin over the lunchroom rabble.

Jaylen checked the answer key. She had correctly identified the organ from the paper diagram spread between them. Becky had dark brown eyes and wore her brunette hair in a short ponytail that bounced behind her head. Jaylen had always appreciated her friendly nature and bubbly personality but didn't find her to be quite the catch that Trip did. He noticed how his friend would stare dreamily in her direction until she turned to him, then Trip would look away and pretend he wasn't watching.

The three of them sat at the end of a lunch table along with Millie Hopkins, a mousy girl with sandy hair who somehow blended into the surroundings and went generally unnoticed until Mr. Kirby assigned her to their group, reminding Jaylen of her existence.

"So, what's the spleen's function?" he asked Becky as a follow-up.

Becky looked at the ceiling and squinted, "Um ... isn't it part of the digestive tract?"

"*BZZZZZ!*" he chided. "Wrong!"

Becky made a pouty face and sighed.

"The spleen filters the blood and participates in various immune functions," Trip said.

"Excellent!" Jaylen said. "You're a brilliant man, Trip Peterson. Isn't that right, Becky?"

"Yeah, he's okay," she said with a twinkle in her eye.

"You want to take a shot at this, Millie Mays?" Jaylen asked.

Millie looked up and shrugged. "I guess."

Before Jaylen could choose a question, a disturbance across the cafeteria drew their attention—a clattering noise followed by a roar of laughter.

Sprawling face-down on the floor with his food and lunch tray scattered before him, lay a skinny kid in an olive-green jacket. A row of khaki-wearing guys with gelled hair sat at a nearby table, leaning over him and chuckling. One of them drew back his ankle from an extended position behind the downed boy's shoes.

The bony kid lifted himself to his knees and wiped mashed potatoes off his cheek. He'd become the star of the hour, top billing in a comedy where everyone in sight pointed at him and laughed. He had every student's attention.

One of the primped boys wearing a peach Polo shirt tossed a wadded napkin at him.

The skinny kid, brown-haired and red-faced, looked slowly around the room. The laughter waned, but most of the crowd still stared and murmured. He brought up one leg in a kneeling position and grabbed his tray with both hands. As he stood, he swung for the fences, smashing it into the head of the guy who'd tripped him.

"Holy crap!" Jaylen said.

The room erupted with *ooohs!* and *ohs!* as the preppy guy clutched his skull and slid onto the floor. Two other Polo shirts leapt from the table and seized Skinny by the lapels. Another guy in an army jacket and sporting a buzzcut appeared from nowhere. He shoved those two off his friend. Then fists went flying. A third boy in a field jacket—a tiny red-haired kid—hovered at the edges, apparently scared to dive in. Bodies crashed to the ground, rolling around and punching. Four or five Polos now outnumbered the green jackets, pounding them viciously. The little guy finally joined the fray, rushed over and kicked a prep in the shin, only to be slugged to the floor by another.

"Fight, fight, fight!" chanted the lunch crowd.

Two male P.E. coaches entered the ring and pulled apart the punching teenagers. They shouted for the Polos to leave but restrained the kids in green who hadn't started the problem in the first place. Yet, those were the ones who were frog-marched out of the cafeteria toward the office.

"Aw, man," Jaylen said. "That ain't fair. Those other kids started it."

"Of course, it's not fair," Becky said. "But those other kids have rich parents. They'll cause headaches for the school if their sons get in trouble. It's easier to pin a fight on the first two."

Trip looked at them both and nodded. He raised his chocolate milk and said, "Life's not fair." Then he finished off the carton.

***

The lunch period on Friday became a time for celebration. The study group had aced Mr. Kirby's anatomy test, and everyone was in high spirits after the gory excitement of the cat dissection. To top it off, over the course of the week, Trip and Becky had kindled a budding romance. The two even had their own private study session the previous afternoon, when Trip treated Becky to a banana split at the Frosty Parlor over on Main Street. Jaylen hadn't been there but imagined their date involved a lot of nervous giggling and maybe some awkward footsie at its spiciest moment.

The group pecked at a tin of homemade brownies Becky had baked for the occasion. Jaylen found himself instantly addicted to the things.

"I'd like to make a toast," he said, swallowing a lump of chocolate. Jaylen stood from his seat and lifted his milk ceremoniously. "To the smartest kids in school ... *us!* Here's to Study Group B. Good job, fellow geniuses!"

The others raised their milks in salute and tapped together their cartons. As they cheered, Trip leaned over to Becky and gave a quick kiss to her cheek. She smiled and blushed.

Jaylen had just stuffed his mouth with more brownie when a noisy distraction caught his attention near the west entrance of the cafeteria. He heard a loud shout followed by a sudden hush. The hush was what Jaylen found odd. Only a special kind of magic could hush a high school lunchroom. He swallowed his brownie.

Just inside the lunchroom doorway, some thirty yards away, stood the skinny boy wearing a green coat and a hateful scowl. He lifted a long, black object. The screams suggested it was a shotgun. The blast erased any doubt.

Mass hysteria swept over the cafeteria. Students tumbled out of their seats and trampled each other to flee.

Millie Hopkins gave a shriek.

"Run!" Jaylen shouted, scrambling around the table for the opposite door. "Run! Run! Get out of here!"

He grabbed Millie's shirt and tugged her along. Trip and Becky were ahead of them, racing hand in hand.

Two more bursts of gunfire cracked from behind. Jaylen saw a kid fall to the floor in a bloody shirt.

Another blast came from a different direction. Screams echoed off the tiled walls, distorting all perception of sound. The rush of panicked teenagers ahead of them suddenly turned tide. The wave of students rushed back in their direction away from the exit and back into the lunchroom, knocking down dozens in the stampede.

A boy with a buzzcut wearing a crooked smirk and an army jacket emerged behind the crowd, blocking the doorway. He raised a monstrous silver revolver with both hands and aimed straight down the barrel.

The boom of the gun clapped through the cafeteria.

Trip and Becky jerked backward.

The bullet ripped through Becky's scalp. She flew off her feet, fingers pulling from Trip's hand. He spun around. His face went bone white.

Jaylen seized Millie by the shoulders and spun her away.

Trip dropped to his knees, leaned over Becky and softly touched her neck.

Another explosion of gunfire, and another kid went down. The buzzcut shooter advanced into the room, blasting at a mob of kids in the center aisles, corralling them toward the buffet area. He wore a shotgun across his back and a second pistol in a holster.

The eastside door was clear.

"The exit!" Jaylen shouted. Blood pumped out of Becky's skull onto the floor. "Run, Trip! It's too late for her! *Run!*" He grabbed both Trip and Millie by their shirts and shot for the doorway, pulling them along.

The nearest exit from the east wing led past the principal's office at the front of school, and that's the direction they ran with a river of frantic people.

Jaylen could see sunlight at the end of the hallway, shining around the corner of a cinderblock wall as they neared the entrance. Then screams erupted from the direction they headed.

POP! POP! POP! POP!

More gunfire blocked the main entrance.

Jaylen's heart fluttered and he felt dizzy. The whole place was cornered at every way out, every turn leading to certain death. A tug on his shirt pulled him off his balance, and he lurched to keep his feet. Now he followed Trip, who stumbled back down the hallway with him and Millie in tow.

POP! POP! POP! from behind them.

BOOM! ... BOOM! from ahead.

Screams soared throughout the school like a ghostly opera.

The trio slipped into a classroom. Trip shot over to a window. Jaylen and Millie followed. The school had been built on a hillside, and they stood at least twenty feet above the parking lot. Even if they broke the glass, a jump would break a leg, at the least. They ran back into the hallway.

POP! POP!

A small ginger kid rounded the front corner. He wore a green field jacket and held a pistol in each hand. Three bodies lay motionless across the floor.

More fleeing students sped past them. No time to think, Jaylen flung open another door, and the three of them tumbled inside, slamming it behind. Trip and Jaylen threw their backs against it. The classroom was otherwise empty.

"He can probably shoot right through the wood," Jaylen said.

Millie slid them a metal chair. Jaylen wedged the chair back beneath the door lever and backed away, praying it would hold.

A powerful boom vibrated through the building, followed by a miserable howl—one of their peers dying in the hall, no doubt. Jaylen leaned against a wall to steady his swimming head.

"I don't want to die!" Millie chirped between whimpers while wringing her hands. Her face pink and puffy, she shifted on her feet like a child who had to pee. "I think Becky's *dead!*" The words came out as a squeak.

POP! POP! The sound drew nearer.

"What are we going to do?!" Millie squealed.

Jaylen scanned the room for a weapon. He saw a map of the world, books, chairs, desks, a wastebasket but nothing easy to wield, and nothing deadly but a sharpened pencil.

And a pad of paper.

Jaylen snatched the last two items from the teacher's desk and rushed them over to Trip. He thrust them both at his friend. "Here!" he said. "Do your stuff!"

The two looked at each other. Trip's gaze was hollow, his eyes empty and adrift. "I don't understand."

"Come on, man!" Jaylen said. "I know you got it in you. You're our only hope. A few more minutes, and we're all gonna die!"

"What do you want me to do?" Trip said, slow and listless.

Jaylen put a hand on Trip's shoulder. "I want you to save us. I want you to write one of your stories."

"What?" Trip said. "A story?"

"Yes! A story. Get it together, man!"

Trip blinked.

"Do it for Becky."

Trip dropped his head. A few seconds later he looked up. Somewhere deep inside his heartbroken friend, Jaylen saw a spark come to life. He placed the pencil in Trip's hand.

"I believe in you," Jaylen said. "Now, let 'em have it!"

IV

Your old man was right.

The red-headed shooter had a name. His drunken dad called him dumbass. His stepmom called him Stupid. The other two green-coats called him Match. Nobody else bothered to learn his name. He lived life as a floor mat, a punching bag or a doorstop, and people didn't tend to use names for things like that.

Today, however, was supposed to be the day he turned the page, and got even with all the assholes who'd ever held him down in the role of unnamable object. And there were a lot of them.

But a funny thing happened on the road to glory. None of the people he'd shot had ever done a damn thing to him. With a gun in each hand—just like in the action movies—he used his dad's nine-millimeters to shoot his favorite teacher, Mrs. Dietz, in the gut. She tried to ask him *why* with her final dying breath.

He shot a girl in the back. When she fell to the floor, he saw a familiar Asian face, a friendly girl who sat near him in history class and always said hello.

Where were the rich kids who ridiculed his looks on a daily basis? Where were the bastards who thought it funny to punch him in the nuts, or to rip off his underpants in gym class and post the video online?

POP! POP! Match shot an old friend through the neck. They used to ride BMX bikes together in the trails off Grayson Drive. They hadn't spoken in a while, but he'd been a decent kid. Now, he laid crumpled in the corner.

He shot a few more victims who limped off or were dragged away. Maybe they died, or maybe they'll just be disfigured or paralyzed. People will surely make fun of their looks and disabilities.

Just like they made fun of you, Match.

Feel better about yourself?

You bastard. You evil piece of shit. You're no vengeful fist of justice, Match. There's no righteousness to your actions. You're the villain in this scenario. The people you've killed are loved by others. These are valuable individuals. They don't deserve to be shot down like this. They possess a value you'll never understand, because you *have no* value. You have nothing positive to offer the world. You haven't evened the score with your enemies. You've only spread your misery to the others around you in the pathetic hope that if you dragged everyone else down to the depths of your despair, then you wouldn't feel so alone.

The truth is, you shrimpy, unlovable coward, is that you didn't have the strength to rise above the worms of the world, so you joined them squirming in the mud. If you had a shred of decency left to offer the human race, then you'd end it all right now. Take out the garbage once and for all.

Match stared down the corridor of the Trapper Valley High hallway, littered with fresh young corpses. No turning back now. He pressed the cold muzzles of both guns to his temples and curled his fingers around the triggers.

Your old man told you time and time again, Match: *Boy, you ain't never gonna amount to nothin'.*

Your old man was right.

***

Trip had attacked the notepad, scrawling madly over the paper. Jaylen couldn't make out the slapdash writing but after just a few lines, Trip block-printed the words THE END in the center of the page.

Double gunshots somewhere up the hallway punctuated the D.

Trip glanced up. "One down."

From the gleam in his friend's eye, Jaylen immediately understood. "That was fast."

"Suicide," Trip said. "The shortest distance between two points."

"What do you mean?" whimpered Millie.

The classroom door shook, followed by pounding. Frightened shouts came from the other side. "Let us in! Oh God, here he *comes!*" More than one person beat on the wood; it sounded like girls.

Gunfire exploded in the distance.

"We've got to let them in!" Jaylen snatched the chair from the door.

He opened it to three crying faces who spilled into the room. Two girls stumbled inward as well as a boy bleeding from his side. The boy rolled to the floor and looked up from a head of shiny gelled hair with blond highlights. The guy who'd tripped the shooter in the lunchroom on Monday had a purple lump on his forehead. And he'd taken a bullet.

Jaylen shook his head. *Prick.*

"I need help," muttered the prick.

Trip shoved the chair back beneath the doorknob to secure the entry.

Jaylen pulled off his sweatshirt and folded it in quarters. He pressed the cloth to the boy's wound to stop the bleeding. The preppy kid howled.

"No whining," Jaylen told him.

"He's shooting everyone!" screeched one of the girls. "It's Ray Benson!"

Jaylen looked down at the prick. "That's your friend from the lunchroom floor. Sounds like he's got some unfinished business with you, and we're all getting in the way." He turned back to the girls. "Where is he?"

Both girls pointed through the wall, and one said, "Biology lab!"

Millie sat crouched in the corner of the room, holding herself and shivering.

Jaylen knew they had only minutes to spare. "Trip. Can you do it again? Same thing?"

Trip frowned. "Not the same. I don't think that will work. But I'll come up with something."

He flipped to a clean sheet of paper. "You said the bio lab?"

***

Ray Benson stalked down the blood-spattered halls, gritting his teeth as he slid four fresh shells into the Remington pump-action, then racked the gun.

They were all going to pay. When the news crews finally broadcast his name across the airwaves, everybody will think to themselves: *My God, that's Ray Benson, the skinny guy we all had fun fucking with. Remember that time in the locker room after P.E. class? Or when we kicked his ass behind the pizza parlor after school? Remember that time we tripped him in the lunchroom? Yeah, that Ray Benson. As it turned out, we picked on the wrong guy, because now everybody's dead. All our friends are dead, so I guess Ray Benson was one guy we shouldn't have fucked with.*

Ray blasted the shotgun through a classroom door. He racked the gun and kicked open the splintered slab. Nothing. The room was empty.

He advanced down the hall, stepping over a dead janitor. The double-doors ahead led through the biology lab and to the east wing. He kicked them open and blasted a shot into dimly lit silence. The pungent smell of formaldehyde tickled his nostrils. He saw no one in the room, but each table held an aluminum pan with a ruined animal carcass.

He prowled through the lab, eyes and ears on highest alert.

The sunlight leaking through the blinds gave the room an eerie glow, glinting off the beakers and steel. Movement caught the corner of his eye. On the opposite side of the lab something shifted just out of view. A strange, low warble came from his left. Then, a scraping sound came from his right.

Ray squinted and lifted the shotgun to line up the sight. If someone were hiding in here, they'd made a huge final mistake. He reached the far wall and put his back against it. Without moving his finger off the trigger, he hit the light switch with his elbow.

The ceiling fluorescents glowed to life.

Ray Benson saw something that simply could not be.

On the table in front of him, the matted hair of a dead cat rippled and pulsated in a dissection pan, wiggling the pins and labels that protruded from its ravaged body. The cat's ruined head rotated creakily to face him with dry, shriveled eyes. The craggy mouth opened and gave an agonized groan.

The nerves in his mind sputtered and blinked. He tried to compute what he saw, but his circuits kept shorting.

More pans stirred as gutted cats rose onto their paws with anguished hisses and growls. A haggard mewling echoed through the room and filled Ray's ears.

Angry dead cats made no sense, yet here they were. Only one explanation...

I've flipped my lid, Ray thought in a stewing panic.

With a metallic clatter, a pan fell from a table-top as a cat crawled free.

Haven't you heard, cats? I'm a guy not to fuck with!

With a pull of the trigger, a cat exploded across the room.

More pans clanged onto the floor tile. Cats leapt from table to table, heading straight for him. Some slinked onto the floor and slid through chair legs to surround him from all sides. Ray's hands trembled around the gunstock.

Steady that trigger finger!

His heart thumped through his chest.

You're cracking up, Ray. Killer cats don't exist.

He pulled the trigger. Another cat flew apart.

The other cats flew at Ray.

Ravenous, frenzied predators, the things were fast and mighty. He elbowed, kicked, spat and cursed. They wre everywhere. A dozen mummified cats sank snapping fangs into his skin and scraped at his eyes with lifeless claws. He clubbed them and smashed them with the gun.

"Get off me! Get off me! *Get offff!*

Slashing his face and neck with razor-sharp nails and steel-trap strength, they tore away his flesh and his resolve. Ray recognized a shrill scream as his own only when it petered to a gurgle when the cats opened his jugular.

His legs folded beneath him. It wasn't supposed to end like this.

Ray had met his match.

Dying on the floor, he watched dead cats lap up his blood like a pool of spilled milk.

***

Trip scratched the words THE END across the bottom of the page, while panting for air as though he'd just a sprinted a mile. "That makes two."

Jaylen saw the circles beneath his eyes. Churning out the stories evidently took a toll on his friend. But after hearing the scuffle and other strange sounds across the hallway, silence followed. The gunman must have been neutralized. The stories must be working.

An electronic chime startled one of the girls, who pulled a mobile phone from her pocket. "Text from Cassie," she told her friend. "She says the school's been evacuated and police have it surrounded."

The view outside the classroom windows was largely obscured by the gymnasium, but Jaylen could see cop cars filing into the south parking lot.

A gunpowder blast cracked somewhere beyond the classroom door.

"The third shooter," Jaylen said.

A crazed cackle came from outside in the hallway. "Calling all boys and girls … I'm coming to *killllllll yooooouuuuuuu!*" taunted the shooter.

"It's Clinton Blake," said the girl with the phone. "I always knew he was a sicko."

Jaylen pulled up a chair to the desk where Trip sat with his head in his hands, catching his breath.

"You've got one more in you. Right, buddy?"

Trip peered through his fingers then dropped his hands. He sat up straight and flipped a page on the notepad. "Right." He lifted his pencil.

***

Clinton Blake was an angel of death. Just ask him.

The other kids in school may have known Blake as that weird, buzzcut kid with the crazed look in his eyes, but the truth was much scarier than fiction.

Now, he stalked the hallways with a wolf-like grin, a loaded twelve-gauge in his hands and a forty-four revolver on his hip. This was his moment and it sizzled with excitement, brimming with an existential energy that Blake knew came only at the pinnacle of one's life, the moment when one fulfills their ultimate destiny. The sheer intensity that pumped through his veins when cutting down his classmates intoxicated him, exalted him and made him crave it ever more. To rein superior over man and beast, over peer and authority, by obliterating all that lay before him—that was Clinton Blake's true calling. Destruction. Devastation. Wanton murder and marvelous mayhem, this was his music and he the conductor. He'd organized the assault. He'd lifted the broken spirits of his fellow teenage soldiers, stoked their angst and given them a cause to believe in.

Now the day was at hand ... and proving to be better than he'd ever expected.

When he struck down his peers, he felt a surge of power he'd never felt from killing a neighborhood dog, or even when he shot his sleeping parents earlier this morning. The thrill of the hunt gave him pleasure like nothing else, and provided the satisfaction he so desperately needed.

"The grim reaper's here to collect!" he called down the hall, searching for signs of life. "I know you're in here! I'm gonna open every door and blow away everyone I see! Say your prayers!"

A drop of sweat trickled down his nose from the beads on his brow. His every sensory nerve buzzed with exhilaration. He walked awkwardly with a diamond-hard erection pushing against his zipper, loving every magnificent second of anticipation. People were nearby, cowering. He could *feel* it.

The bodies strewn on the hallway floor lay still. He kicked open a door to his right. Desks inside were knocked over and papers scattered, but no one in sight.

Sirens wailed outside. From the sound, an army of police vehicles had swarmed the school.

Blake stepped back out of the classroom, floating the shotgun barrel hungrily in front of him. "I'm going to blow holes in your body and then *laaaauugh* and *laaaaaauugh* as I watch you die!" He snickered as he said this. He knew they heard him, wherever they were.

He kicked open the door across the hall.

Nothing. A glass globe of the world sat on the teacher's desk. He thought of blasting it apart then decided to save the ammo for something juicier.

Twenty feet down the hall on his right, the lab door hung open with a body piled in the entryway. Blake saw the butt of a shotgun beside it and crept over to investigate.

Ray Benson lay dead with his flesh scored by countless razor cuts. A deep wound gaped from his neck. Blood swamped the floor around him, and a bunch of gored, withered cat carcasses cluttered the surrounding area.

Bizarre, thought Blake. He bent closer and snapped a mental photo. *Surreal and Beautiful.* He smiled and moved on.

The faintest sound of movement met his ears from the classroom across the hall. Someone hid behind that door. Clinton Blake's mouth watered. The time had come for another kill, and a tingle ran through him.

He racked the gun.

A voice on a loudspeaker crackled outside. The police, of course. *Come on in and I'll shoot you, too*, Blake thought.

In his periphery, a figure appeared in the shadows at the mouth of the hallway. He tried to ignore it. The girl lurching down the corridor toward him was dead, and he couldn't be bothered. Right now, a terrified student—maybe more than one—waited just beyond this classroom door, and Blake needed to focus. He needed to kill them and would not be distracted.

At the opposite end of the hallway, more figures slowly rose from the piles on the floor, broken and dripping. They staggered toward him.

"I know you're in there!" Blake screamed at the door, his palms sweaty and his sights centered on whoever would be revealed whenever he kicked it open.

He scanned his perimeter. The rising victims had increased in number, and the blood-covered shapes moaned and shambled in his direction. Some were shorn of limbs, others spilled their innards. A horde of the things were closing in on him. Their eyes, flat and empty, floated in their faces as lifeless baggage.

Focus, damn it!

His mind tended to play tricks sometimes.

He returned to the door and aimed.

"Let's have some fun, people! *Ha-ha-hah!*"

Clinton Blake pulled the trigger.

***

Jaylen gasped as the door latch exploded from the jamb. He covered his face, and debris pelted his hands. The wedged chair tumbled to the side. The door slung open with the kick of a boot. The shooter burst inside and racked the gun.

Jaylen saw a green coat and a black muzzle. It flashed with a *boom!* Phone girl twisted and crashed into a row of desks. Millie screamed from the corner.

The shooter racked again, and spread a crazed smile as he stared at Jaylen with eyes ablaze. Jaylen looked down into the dark void of an enormous shotgun barrel. He thought of his mother and of God.

The shooter yelped. The gun tilted, firing into the ceiling. Several groping hands grabbed the boy from behind, jerking his limbs backward and wrenching away the gun. Clinton Blake's eyes bugged wide. He crowed hysterically, screaming and laughing as the throng of dead students overtook him from behind. They pulled him down and tore at him with their teeth and fingers.

Becky Morgan, pale as cotton, led the charge. A ragged flap of scalp bounced behind her peeled skull, weighted by her sporty little pony tail. She raked at Blake's face with one hand and sank the other into his abdomen. The angry corpses stretched the skin of his doughy torso so tight it split open to show his pink muscle and yellow fat. The stench of bile flooded the room. Blake gagged and thrashed as the throng of victims feasted on his meat, and Becky stirred inside his guts. She twisted her wrist and ripped out his spleen. She held it high to her surviving friends for approval, presenting the prize with a wicked grin to Study Group B.

Jaylen and Trip gaped at each other, and then at Millie. They all stared at the glistening organ—which filters blood and participates in various immune functions—and they fainted.

***

Mass murder leaves a town peaceful in its wake. That was Jaylen Reynolds's experience. Grief brought with it a sweeping calm.

A town in mourning, Trapper Valley took a rest after the initial shock, with quieter streets, less hustle and bustle. The schools all closed the following week, funerals were held, and the churches were packed. People stayed mostly in their homes, comforting each other and reflecting on life's fragile nature. A sense of kinship fostered among the townies, if only for a moment, in which people put aside their differences and embraced the community.

The news reporters had a million questions. Everyone did.

A couple of kids had the answers.

But Jaylen wasn't talking, even though he remembered every grisly detail.

He'd awakened unharmed on a stretcher that day with his mother at his side. He stayed by her side the next several days in a row.

Once school finally came back in session, the students fell back into routine. The athletes hung out with the athletes. The metal-heads, the preppy kids and the hipsters all reformed their teams.

Jaylen found himself alone again. Trip didn't show up that first day back, or the second. After a week, Jaylen gave up hope. He figured that after all the violence his friend now viewed Trapper Valley as just another ugly memory—tainted, like his other schools—and had convinced his parents once again to let him move on.

Kind of a bummer. High school would be much less magical without him.

But Jaylen chose not to see Trip's decision to leave as a sad end to the saga. In fact, he hoped to run into the guy again one day. He viewed his friend's departure as only the end of a chapter, just a pause in a larger story, because Jaylen knew, deep down, there was so much more to be written.

And he was unwilling to wait for someone else to do the job.

So, one Friday afternoon, while sitting on the porch of his house, Jaylen took out a spiral notepad and a Number Two pencil. He looked at the blue-lined sheet and thought for a moment. Then he touched the graphite to the paper and went to work.

The End

<u>**Story Notes**</u>

"Incident at the Buttered Biscuit" appeared in *Seven Feet Under* published by Sinister Grin Press, 2016.

"Dammit, Mavis" appeared in *Creature Stew* published by Papa Bear Press, 2015.

"Code Black" appeared in *Welcome to the Splatter Club Vol. 1* published by Blood Bound Books, 2020.

"Vampire Lake" appeared in *Dead & Bloated* published by The Evil Cookie Publishing, 2023.

"Bad Brunch in the Big Easy" appeared in *Seven Feet Under* published by Sinister Grin Press, 2016.

"Silver Bullet Lies" appears here in *Killed By Death* for the first time, 2024.

"In the Shadows of the Trees" appeared in *Seven Feet Under* published by Sinister Grin Press, 2016.

"Beware the Whammy" appeared in *Double Barrel Horror Vol. 1* published by Pint Bottle Press, 2016.

"Men of Their Word" appeared on the *Splatter Club* blog, published by Blood Bound Books at www.bloodgutsandstory.com, 2022.

"To Kill a Guy Twice" appeared in *Ghosts' Revenge* published by James Ward Kirk Publishing, 2015.

"Hell Comes to the Burger Hut" appeared in *Welcome to the Splatter Club Vol. 2* published by Blood Bound Books, 2021.

"Bloodbath in First Grade" was produced as an audio drama for *The Wicked Library*, Episode 817: Extra Wicked Summer Anthology, 2018.

"Let 'em Have It" appeared in *Seven Feet Under* published by Sinister Grin Press, 2016.

About the Author

Matthew Weber lives in Alabama where he is husband to a beautiful wife and father of three awesome kids. He makes his living by editing various construction magazines and he writes scary stories out of love for the horror genre. When he's not chasing his children or pecking at his laptop, he plays bass for the long-running punk band Skeptic? You can find more about Weber's fiction at www.pintbottlepress.com and find Skeptic? at www.skepticmusic.com.